**Deadly ambush . . .**

Both helicopters opened fire on Nhu and his men, and Phat saw Nhu and the others dive off the dike and splash down into the flooded paddy. Automatic-weapons fire coming from the vegetation across the paddy told Phat that he was correct in his belief that the Americans would be waiting in a blocking position. As Phat stared across the paddy, he saw scores of American soldiers coming out of the trees, moving toward Nhu and his men.

The helicopter Phat had hit turned and started down toward the paddy to make an emergency landing. Phat fired again at the helicopter, and he saw the front windshield of the ship fill with holes as his bullets sprayed into it. The helicopter, which had been coming down in a smooth descent, suddenly lurched and fell over on its side. It crashed hard, then exploded into a great, greasy ball of flame.

## DATELINE: AN LOI

# DATELINE: AN LOI

**ERNIE CHAPEL**

*PaperJacks* LTD.

TORONTO    NEW YORK

AN ORIGINAL

*PaperJacks*

DATELINE: AN LOI

*PaperJacks* LTD

330 STEELCASE RD. E., MARKHAM, ONT. L3R 2M1
210 FIFTH AVE., NEW YORK, N.Y. 10010

**First edition published February 1988**

This is a work of fiction in its entirety. Any resemblance to actual people, places or events is purely coincidental.

ISBN 0-7701-0711-7
Copyright © 1988 by Robert Vaughan
All rights reserved
Printed in the USA

# DATELINE: AN LOI

# Prologue

The day was scorching, at least ninety-five degrees, and a hot, dusty wind rattled the limbs of the cottonwood trees. The road ran alongside a riverbed, dry except for a narrow stream of slow-moving muddy water. On both sides of the narrow stream the mud had caked and broken into a mosaic of crazy tile.

Ernie Chapel was in southwestern South Dakota, in the area known as the Badlands. Here, on rubble-strewn barrens, or shale land, under the overhangs of rocky plateaus, or in eroded gullies, he could see prickly pear and sage weed growing alongside the beautiful and delicate penstemon, and Indian paintbrush. This was home to prairie dogs, buffalo, and pronghorn antelopes.

Ernie had the hood of his van propped open, as

he walked down the side of the riverbank toward the narrow stream that ran through the middle. Behind him, little wisps of steam curled up from the radiator. He was carrying an empty milk carton.

Ernie dipped water from the middle of the stream, then walked back up to the van. It had cooled down enough for him to pop off the radiator cap, and this he did. A little water gushed over, but not too much. He waited for a moment, then poured the water from the milk carton into the radiator.

He was just coming back up the hill for the fourth time when a pickup truck pulled up behind his van. Though not rotating, there was a blue light on top of the truck, and a sign on the door read: INDIAN POLICE, PINE RIDGE RESERVATION. A tall, dark-skinned, dark-eyed Indian got out of the truck and walked toward the van. He was wearing khaki trousers and a khaki shirt. His blue-black hair hung down his back in a long braid. A star was pinned to his pocket and a pistol was strapped to his side.

"I hope you're straining that water," the Indian policeman said. "Otherwise, it's so dirty it could pollute your entire cooling system."

"I had to do something to cool the block down," Ernie replied. "My engine was about to go belly-up on me, and that wouldn't be too good out here." He leaned against the van and wiped his forehead. His beard and hair were white, his eyes blue.

"No, you're a long way from anywhere," the Indian said. He eyed Ernie curiously. "Are you visiting someone on the reservation?"

"Yes," Ernie said.

"Who? Maybe I can help you . . . give you some directions how to get there."

"An old friend of mine," Ernie said. He slid open the door to the side of his van, opened the little refrigerator, and took out two cold cans of beer. He handed one to the Indian policeman, then popped the top off his own.

"I'm on duty, I can't drink this," the Indian said. Even as he spoke he popped the top, then took a long swallow.

"Yeah, I shouldn't be drinking and driving either," Ernie said. "But I'm not exactly driving right now. I'm looking for Hunter Two Bears."

"What do you want to see Two Bears for?" the policeman asked.

"I just want to talk to him."

"You know Hunter Two Bears?" the Indian asked.

"Yes."

The Indian paused with the beer can halfway to his lips. He squinted at Ernie.

"How come you know him? You a federal marshal?"

"No. I'm just a private citizen."

"When's the last time you saw Hunter Two Bears?" the Indian wanted to know.

"I'd say it's been eighteen years."

"Eighteen years? Eighteen years ago Hunter was in Vietnam."

"I know."

"You a Vietnam vet?" the Indian asked.

"No, but I was there." Ernie stuck out his hand. "My name is Ernie Chapel."

The Indian policeman smiled broadly. "Ernie Chapel? You're the one wrote the stories about Hunter, aren't you? You're the one got him his medal."

"No," Ernie said quickly. "Yes, I did write the stories, but I had nothing to do with his getting the medal. He did that all on his own."

The Indian finished his can of beer, then put it on the floorboard of Ernie's van. "Throw that outside and I'm going to arrest you for littering," he said, pointing to the can. He hitched up his trousers. "Think this thing will run now?"

"I'm sure it will," Ernie answered.

"Come on, follow me. I'll take you to Two Bears."

Ernie thanked the policeman, then put the hood down on his van. When he started the engine, he was gratified to see that it started with no difficulty. The pickup truck drove by. Then Ernie pulled out on the road to follow him.

For over ten years, Ernie Chapel had covered the Vietnam experience, from the murder of the Diems to the helicopters the Vietnamese crash-landed at sea in the early days. He had been a reporter for Combined Press International, writing stories for the newspapers back home.

Ernie had seen it all in Vietnam, from the bloody booby traps on the My Kahn Floating Restaurant to the Phantom Jet raids on Hanoi. He had dined with the loveliest women Vietnam had to offer, and he had shared foxholes with dying soldiers. Now he was retired, travelling around the country, renewing old relationships and tying up loose ends. It was just such a task that brought him to the Pine Ridge Indian Reservation in South Dakota.

Ernie followed the pickup truck. Because his engine had already overheated oncv, he was running without the air conditioner. The windows were down and hot wind blew through the van. He looked around the barren hills and desolate land. So, this was where Hunter Two Bears came from. Ernie smiled. He understood Hunter a little better now. It would take a mean son of a bitch to survive this place, and Hunter Two Bears was about as mean as they came.

# Chapter One

Viet Cong Attack Long Binh.

By Ernie Chapel

LONG BINH, South Vietnam, NOV. 7, 1967 — Viet Cong guerrillas staged mortar and sapper attacks last night against United States soldiers at the sprawling military base at Long Binh.

Two Americans were killed and eleven were wounded in the shellings, a headquarters spokesman said. The attack was aimed at the 90th Replacement Depot, and at those soldiers who had either just arrived, or were just leaving Vietnam.

The United States headquarters official said over 150 rounds of enemy mortar fire struck the base, while at least two dozen sappers attempted to sneak on to the base to plant explosives. More than a dozen of the sappers were killed. Estimates are that another dozen VC were killed by "Puff the Magic Dragon" in defense of the base. "Puff the Magic Dragon" is a C-130 cargo plane, armed along one side with a row of miniguns. These guns, with rotating barrels similar to the old "Gatling" guns of the Civil War era, are capable of firing 550 rounds per minute. Ten such guns are located throughout the ship, firing through the windows at the ground below. A gunner tends to the guns, while the airplane orbits just out of range of ground fire. It is said that one of these planes can put a bullet in every square foot of a football field during just one minute of firing. . . .

"To hell with it, Sarge," Sergeant Bill Hanlon said.

"Yeah, really," Sergeant First Class Hunter Two Bears answered.

Ernie burped, then took another swallow of his beer. "To hell with them all," he added.

"Except for six, and save them for pallbearers," Bill put in.

SFC Hunter Two Bears, Sergeant Bill Hanlon, and Ernie Chapel were sitting on top of a bunker at Long Binh, drinking beer and discussing ways to end the war.

"The way I see it," Bill went on, "we ought to put Nixon and Ho Chi Minh on a deserted island somewhere . . . without any weapons of any kind, without clothes, even."

"Without clothes?" Hunter asked.

"Yeah. You know, strip them down to their bare essence."

Ernie laughed. "Can't you just see Nixon and Ho Chi Minh with their bare essences hanging out?"

"I think it would make a fine sight," Hunter said. "To their bare *ass*ences," he toasted.

"We ought to just put them there and say, 'Okay, we'll be back in six hours to pick up whoever's left alive.' "

Hunter burped, then punched a hole in the top of another beer can. "That's what we need: young, fresh ideas like that."

Ernie laughed. "And what then?" he asked.

"What then?" Bill replied. He took a long swallow of his beer. "Well, hell, it's simple," he said. "When we go back we just kill whichever son of a bitch is left alive and get on about our business."

There was a stomach-shaking boom from across the base and a huge ball of fire rose into a night sky that was already criss-crossed with tracer rounds.

"Son of a bitch!" someone shouted from down inside the bunker. "Did you hear that? That was close!"

" 'Course, if you put those two pussies together, you sure wouldn't have much of a fight," Hunter noted, paying absolutely no attention to the shouts of panic from the bunker, nor to the fire fight going on across the base.

"Do you . . . do you think the security team can stop them?" a frightened voice asked.

"God, I hope so. I'm a personnel clerk. I'm not supposed to have to worry about this shit."

Hunter had driven Bill down to Long Binh today. Bill, who had been one of Hunter's squad leaders, had finished his twelve months and was taking the Freedom Bird back to the world the next morning. Ernie had met both of them in the NCO club a little earlier. He wanted to go up-country to do a story, so Hunter invited him to go back with him the next day. Tonight they were giving Bill a royal send-off.

In the meantime a suicide squad of VC sappers had chosen that very night to attack Long Binh. When the attack came, everyone rushed to the bunkers except Bill, Hunter, and Ernie. They took a couple of six-packs of beer to the top of the bunker they were assigned to, and throughout the attack they sat there watching the show. They felt no sense of danger, because the attack was taking place a good half mile away from them.

"Well, it's not like you could sell tickets to watch them or anything," Bill defended. "That's not what it's about. Who'd want to watch two wimps fight?"

From some point in the sky a solid stream of red tracer rounds started streaming down toward the ground.

"Look at that, will you?" Ernie said, pointing to the sky. "They brought in Puff."

"So, that's Puff," Bill observed. "Shit! No wonder nobody can get Puff up-country. He's too busy down here protecting file clerks."

"Come on, Bill, don't be so hard on file clerks,"

Hunter said. "You're going home tomorrow, aren't you? Just think if Charlie got in and screwed up all the records and nobody knew when anyone's DROS was."

"Yeah, you're right."

"DROS, R&R, payday. That's what we're fighting for."

"Maybe that's what you old farts are fighting for," Bill said. "But not me."

"What are you fighting for?"

"A twenty-two-foot jumper at the buzzer, root-beer floats, screwin' on the beach."

"Really? You think Custer's men were fighting for that shit when my people kicked his ass?" Hunter asked.

"Nah. They didn't have basketball then," Bill said.

"No, but they had beaches and they sure as hell had screwin'," Ernie said.

The sound of Puff's guns reached them. They didn't pop like machine guns; they buzzed like a buzz saw.

Hunter held his beer can up to the sky in salute. "Give 'em hell, Puff."

"Yeah, pour it on 'em," Bill said.

There were three louder-than-nomral bangs as, over by the perimeter where Charlie was trying to make his penetration, three Claymores were set off.

"Oh, shit! Did you hear that?" a frightened voice down in the bunker said. "Those were Claymores! They must be gettin' through for the Claymores to be set off!"

"What if they come over here?"

"Where's the goddamned security? Goddammit! Why aren't they doin' their job?"

A Viet Cong mortar went to work and a round was dropped in one of the company streets.

"Oh, shit! Now they're using mortars!" someone down in the bunker said.

"You think this bunker can take a direct hit?"

"I don't know, I wouldn't want to find out."

"What about those three dumb shits up on top?"

"To hell with them. Two of 'em are from up-country, the other one's a reporter who doesn't even have to be here. If you ask me, they're all three crazy."


"Hey, Bill, you goin' to stay in the army?" Hunter asked. "I mean you're what, twenty? And already made sergeant. Hell, I was twenty-five before I made my third stripe. It seems a shame for you to just go home and throw it away."

"I don't know, man," Bill answered. "I've got a basketball scholarship to go to college. Seems like I ought to try and make something of myself."

"You can make something of yourself in the army," Hunter said.

Bill laughed. "Trying to work the old recruitment on me, are you, Sarge?"

"It's an honorable profession."

"Yeah, well, you Indians always have been big on that honor shit," Bill said.

"What do you know about Indians?" Hunter asked.

"Hell, I read *Last of the Mohicans*, and I know all about Tonto, and, oh, I saw the movie *Broken*

*Arrow.* That was a damned good flick, man, with Jimmy Stewart? He married an Indian girl in that picture.''

"Damn! With credentials like that, the government could appoint you head of the B.I.A.," Ernie teased.

"You got that right." Hunter laughed. He rubbed his chin. "Say, listen," he said, suddenly changing the subject. "Are you two guys hungry? Would you like some steak?''

"Steak? Are you serious?" Ernie asked.

"Sure," Hunter answered. "When we walked by the officers' club before this shit started, I saw a bunch of doofus lieutenants cooking steaks. What you just bet they're still on the grill? If we don't get them, they'll burn up.''

"Make mine well done," Bill said.

"Hell, at this point they're all well done," Hunter replied.

"Come on, Ernie, we'll go get more beer," Bill suggested.

The three men climbed down from the bunker. Then, as Ernie and Bill went to get more beer, Hunter moved along the fence line toward the officers' club, where he had seen the cookout. He was right about the steaks being left on the grill, because he could smell the cooked meat.

Hunter sensed it, more than he saw it . . . a quiet sound, an almost imperceptible shadow down inside the rolled, concertina wire that lay at the base of the perimeter fence. Hunter made no sign that he had seen or heard anything. He didn't look toward the fence, not even the slightest glance. Instead, he continued walking with the same, nonchalant stride with which he had begun. Then, when he was a few feet beyond the shadow, he let himself look back.

There, lying very still, was a Vietnamese in the black pajamalike uniform worn by the V.C. This V.C. was on his stomach and moving slowly, right down the middle of the roll of concertina wire, totally oblivious to the barbs. He was pushing a satchel in front of him, and Hunter knew that the satchel must be loaded with explosive.

It wasn't too hard to figure out the V.C.'s mission. While his friends were making a demonstration across the base and creating enough action to bring all the security teams on Long Binh, plus Puff, this guy was sneaking around to the other side to plant a satchel charge where it would do the most good, such as in an enlisted barracks or BOQ. Maybe he would just throw the charge into the nearest bunker.

Whatever the mission, Hunter knew from his experience with them up-country that Charlie had a good chance of accomplishing it. That was because the typical V.C. sapper was tough and skilled enough to move through barbed wire without even slowing down. He was also dedicated enough to his cause to give up his life in the effort.

*Okay, you son of a bitch*, Hunter thought. *I'll help you give up your life.*

The V.C. knew, of course, that Hunter was there. The advantage was in the fact that the V.C. didn't know that Hunter knew about him. Quickly, and catching the V.C. totally by surprise, Hunter stepped into the concertina wire and brought the heel of his boot down sharply on the V.C.'s wrist. He felt the bones go under his heel, and he saw the V.C.'s hand open up involuntarily as he released his grip on the satchel.

Hunter reached down and picked up the satchel charge, then tossed it over the fence as far as he could. It exploded harmlessly out in an adjacent rice paddy.

"Jeez! Did you hear that?" someone back in the bunker said. "That was close!"

Hunter grabbed the V.C. by the back of his neck and dragged him up, right through the concertina wire. The V.C. came up with a knife in his other hand and he made a wild, slashing motion, which, if it had caught Hunter, would have disemboweled him. The V.C. had the advantage of a weapon and desperation. Hunter, though really not much larger than the V.C., had the advantage of strength and two good hands. Neither he nor the V.C. made a sound as they engaged in their life-and-death struggle.

The V.C. slashed at him again but Hunter counterpunched, going in right over the V.C.'s wild swing. He caught the V.C. on the point of his chin and the V.C. went down on the concertina. The V.C. made a gasp, followed by a gurgling noise, and Hunter didn't understand why until he saw the steel stake. The stake was driven into the ground at an angle, sharpened to prevent attackers from throwing their body onto the concertina and thus providing a mat for others to cross. Hunter's adversary fell on the stake and it came all the way through his body, protruding from the front as a bright, red spear.

"I'll give you this," Hunter said under his breath. "You were a gutsy little shit."

Hunter brushed his hands on his trousers, then went on to do what he had started to do.

The steaks were on a grill that had been built on a concrete pad right outside an officers' club. The coals were still hot, and though the steaks had been moved to one side of the grill when the attack came, they were still close enough to the heat to be cooking, and their rich, succulent aroma filled the air.

There had evidently been a party of some sort going on, because in addition to the steaks there were bowls of fresh fruit, freshly baked bread, and several bottles of liquor. When the attack started, everyone had run to the bunker, leaving all this wonderful food and drink unattended.

Leisurely, Hunter walked over to the grill. There were a dozen or more thick, brown steaks, crisscrossed with grill marks. He picked up the long-handled fork and moved them around until he found three he wanted. Then he took three more for good measure. He took a couple of plates, forks and knives, grabbed a loaf of French bread, then went back to the bunker. Bill and Ernie were already back.

"What took you so long?" Bill asked.

"I found a Charlie sneaking along the fence line," Hunter replied.

"Damn! That looks good," Bill said, seeing the steaks and the French bread. "So, did you take care of him?"

"Yeah," Hunter answered without elaboration. He opened a can of beer that was so cold ice was still clinging to the outside. "Can you believe it?" he asked. "These people here actually drink their beer cold."

"Yeah," Bill answered. "I guess I better get used to that. That's the way it is back in the world, as I remember."

"Seems to me like I recall that as well," Hunter said.

"Hey, listen!" Ernie said.

"Listen to what? I don't hear anything," Hunter replied, chewing a bite of steak.

"That's just it," Ernie said. "The shooting has stopped."

"Well, we must've beaten back the red menace," Bill suggested.

"Careful there," Hunter joked. "Time was when I was the red menace."

A moment later the generators started again and all the perimeter lights that had been turned off during the VC attack went back on. Immediately after the perimeter lights went on, the lights in the barracks, BOQ's, and clubs came on, and that was followed by music. Bill could hear Neil Diamond singing "Sweet Caroline."

"Hey! Hey, it's over, you guys!" someone shouted. "Come on out, it's over!"

"Yeah," another said. "I guess we whipped their asses good."

The officers who were grilling steaks came out of their bunker as well.

"Carl? Carl, how many steaks did we have on this grill?" one of them called.

"A dozen, I think. Why?"

"Son of a bitch! Somebody took half of our steaks."

"Who the hell would take steaks in the middle of a mortar attack? You must have forgot to put the other half on, that's all."

"How the hell do you think they got their commission?" Hunter asked, laughing, as steak juice ran down his chin. "They can't even count."

"You know how it is with the war 'n' all," Ernie answered. "They'll take anyone they can get."

"Hey! Hey, ever'body, look at this!" someone shouted excitedly. "Here's a damned gook hung up on a steel stake! He must've fallen on it tryin' to get in! What do you think about that?"

"We sure are lucky. If he hadn't tripped, he could've made it to our bunker easy. Look how close it is."

"No, we aren't the ones lucky, man. Look at those three dumb shits sittin' up there on top of the bunker, eating and drinking like they don't have a care in the world. They're the ones lucky. They were up there during this whole attack."

"Lucky? They're not lucky. They're crazy."

# Chapter Two

Ernie stood with Hunter as they watched Bill and the other returning G.I.'s load onto the Freedom Bird for the flight home. The returning soldiers were all in khakis, their ribbons making a splash of color on the otherwise drab uniforms. For most of them it was the first time they had been out of fatigues in over a year, and they moved awkwardly in the now unfamiliar dress uniforms. At the top of the mounting ramp, Bill turned and smiled, then flipped the entire base "the bird."

"I've observed that one of the hardest things about being over here is telling friends good-bye," Ernie said. "He seemed like a nice guy."

"Yeah, I'm going to miss the son of a bitch," Hunter said. "You try not to get too close to anybody. Soon as you do, they either get blown away or their time's up and they go back home. At least this one had a happy ending. Damn, I'm hungry. What say we get a little breakfast before we start for An Loi?"

"Fine by me, but it's my treat," Ernie offered. "It's the least I can do to pay you for taking me with you."

"Can't beat that. What I don't understand is why you want to go to An Loi. That's the asshole of the world."

Ernie laughed. "I've heard that same appellation applied to a dozen other places."

"Yeah, I guess so. Being a reporter, I guess you get around quite a bit, don't you?"

"It's my job," Ernie said. He smiled. "On the other hand, it also allows me to leave if things get too bad."

"Yeah, well, An Loi isn't like Omaha Beach, or Iwo Jima, or anything like that. But it's not like the Vietnam these straphangers down here know, either. Where you want to eat?"

"Anywhere you want. After all, you did buy dinner last night."

Hunter thought of the steaks they had eaten and he laughed. "Yeah, those guys couldn't count worth a shit, but they did cook a good steak. There's a little place just outside the gate that we might try."

"You're talking about the Blue Diamond?" Ernie asked.

Hunter laughed. "I see you've been there before."

"Like the songs says, I been everywhere."

The Blue Diamond was five hundred meters

north of the gate on the east side of the road. It was in the middle of a little row of hooches and shops, most of which were showing their wares on shelves out front. Jungle fatigues, boots, canteens, web belts, and other G.I.-issue items were displayed openly, unashamedly, right alongside the dolls, velvet paintings, plastic utensils, cheap watches, and fake jewelry.

They were greeted by a dozen children who pulled on their arms and pants legs, entreating them to buy, or give money.

"If the V.C. recruit their soldiers from these little shits, I can see why they got such guts," Hunter said. "We can have the damnedest fire fight you ever saw, and one minute later kids are out polishing up the brass. It's a wonder more of them don't get killed."

The restaurant smelled good inside. It smelled of fried ham and bacon, fish, savory Oriental spices, pepper, vinegar, and *nuc mahm*. A smiling old woman met them, and she motioned them to a table.

"Shit!" Hunter said. "Last time I was in here there were a lot of pretty girls waiting tables.

"Must have been afternoon," Ernie suggested.

"Yeah, come to think of it, it was. What's that got to do with it?"

"You're up-country, you aren't wise to the ways of the big-city girls," Ernie said with a chuckle. "All the pretty girls are sleeping now."

"Why?"

"Think about it, Hunter. Most of them work until four or five in the morning."

"Oh, yeah," Hunter said. He sighed. "I guess

you're right. Well, I didn't really have time for anything like that, anyway. All I want is something to eat, then get on back. I've got a night patrol to take out."

The men ordered spring rolls, fried rice, noodle soup, fried ham, *bun mae*, and coffee. Ernie doctored his rice and spring rolls with *nuc mahm*.

"You mean you can eat that shit?" Hunter said, commenting about the pungent sauce.

"It takes awhile to get used to, I'll admit," Ernie said. "But I like it now."

"I'll stick to soy sauce and hot peppers," Hunter said.

The first part of the trip back to An Loi was up Highway 1. Highway 1 was wide, well paved, and crawling with as much traffic as any major highway anywhere. Jeeploads of American M.P.'s and Vietnamese Q.C.'s zipped up and down the highway, their long antennae bent by the wind. With the white-striped Jeeps and helmet liners giving them authority, they whipped in and out of traffic as if it were their sacred right to do so. They owned the roads in the same way highway patrolmen owned the roads in the States.

Ernie and Hunter were talking about the army, and the fact that Hunter was "going for his twenty."

"I look around and see all these kids," Hunter was saying. "Most of them hate the army; they count the days until they can get out. They think all they got to do is walk right out into the world with their arms spread wide and some high-paying job's gonna fall right into their laps."

"It's their youth," Ernie suggested.

"Yeah, maybe," Hunter said. "Or, maybe that's just what kids learn in the outside world."

"Outside world? You mean civilians?"

"No. I mean outside world, rather than the reservation."

"Oh."

"I'm Sioux," Hunter explained. "Born and raised on the Pine Ridge Reservation, not too far from Wounded Knee. You ever heard of Wounded Knee?"

"Can't say that I have."

"The last battle between my people and the whites was fought there," Hunter said. He laughed, a bitter, scoffing laugh. "Some battle. My people sat on the ground while the soldiers massacred them. My great-grandfather was killed; my grandfather lost an arm."

"Damn. Don't you sometimes feel a little like a traitor, being in the army?"

"Nah. This army isn't that army. And this army's my home. I enlisted in the middle fifties . . . March of '55, to be exact. I belong in the army. Here, I'm part of something, something bigger than myself. Can you understand?"

"Yes, I understand," Ernie said.

"What was there for me back home? Work in a service station or garage, maybe? Tend sheep, or cattle? No, that wasn't for me. And it's not that I make more money in the army. Fact is, I could own my own service station, or my own cows, and I'd probably make more than I do now. I'm a soldier not for the money . . . but because it's what I am, it's what I'm about. Hell, I know I'm not supposed to admit this, but I'm even enjoying this damned war. After twelve years of training it was like being all dressed up with no place to go. Vietnam gave me a place to go. I've been here for three tours."

"The army's sent you back two times?"

"Sent me back, hell; I haven't left," Hunter said. "I've voluntarily extended each tour."

"Then you really do like it, don't you?" Ernie asked.

"Yeah, well, it isn't just that. The way I figure it, it takes at least a year to learn your way around and another year to know the people. You aren't worth a shit until your third year. Then you're mean and green."

"And that's you, huh? Mean and green?"

"You goddamned right," Hunter said. "Here's our turnoff."

They left Highway 1 and traveled no more than two hundred meters when they saw an M.P. Jeep sitting at the side of the road. As they approached the Jeep, one of the M.P.'s got out and signaled for them to stop.

"What's up?" Hunter asked, as the M.P. stepped up to them.

"Where you headed, Sarge?"

"I'm going to An Loi," Hunter said.

"Who's this?" the M.P. gestured toward Ernie.

"I'm Ernie Chapel," Ernie said. He pulled out his I.D. and press credentials for the M.P. to see. "I have clearance from MACV."

The M.P. looked at the credentials for a moment, then handed them back. He stroked his chin.

"We just got word that a V.C. patrol is working

the road up ahead," the M.P. said. "They may be setting up an ambush."

"Yeah, well, that's what they do," Hunter said.

"What I'm getting at is, you may want to wait until another few vehicles come along. Then you can go with the convoy."

"No, thanks. I'd rather take my chances alone."

"Just a minute," the M.P. said. He walked over toward his own Jeep and spoke to the other M.P. That was when Hunter noticed the other M.P. was a second lieutenant. The second lieutenant nodded his head, then got out and came back toward Hunter. Hunter saluted him as he approached, and the lieutenant returned it.

"Specialist Anderson tells me you don't want to wait for a convoy to be formed."

"No, sir," Hunter said.

"Why not? It would be safer."

"Who figured that out?"

"What do you mean?"

"Lieutenant, if you were a V.C. in charge of two or three men on a suicide mission like this, who would you rather attack? One single Jeep, or a convoy?"

The lieutenant thought for a moment. "Well, I'd want to make it count," he said. "I'd probably wait for a convoy. But that's different."

"Why? You think the V.C. are too dumb to figure that out?"

The lieutenant sighed, then stepped back away from the Jeep. "All right, Sergeant, go ahead," he agreed. "But don't say I didn't warn you."

"Thanks," Hunter said. He shifted into gear and drove away, leaving the lieutenant and SP-4 standing in the road behind him.

"You got a weapon, Ernie?" Hunter asked as they drove away.

"No. I'm a noncombatant. If I get caught with a weapon, my credentials will be pulled."

"Yeah? Well, if we're hit, throw your credentials at them."

Ernie looked around at the rice paddies and thick groves that crowded down to the road. This route, unlike Highway 1 was narrow and winding, with dozens of blind spots and hundreds of opportunities for ambuscade.

"I guess I see what you mean," Ernie replied.

Hunter unsnapped the leg pocket on his jungle fatigues, then pulled out a German P-38 pistol. He handed the weapon to Ernie.

"I bought this while I was in Germany," he said. "I'm not supposed to carry a personal weapon, but it's a sweet little piece and I like having it around."

"Thanks," Ernie said. He held the gun in his lap.

A three-quarter-ton truck went around them. It wasn't actually a truck — the truck body had been removed and all that remained was the engine, chassis, seat, and steering wheel. The driver, a Vietnamese soldier, was wearing goggles and a long purple scarf. The scarf fluttered wildly in the wind. He was driving nearly seventy miles an hour, and within a moment he was already around the next turn and out of sight.

"Think he's not about to turn a buck?" Hunter

laughed. "There will be a bus body on that chassis by this time tomorrow, and he'll be five hundred dollars richer."

"1 A-V-N B-G-D-E," Ernie read from the rear bumper. "1 Bn, A-14."

"Ha! I know the motor sergeant in that battalion," Hunter said. "Think I'll ask him if he's missing a three-quarter."

The sound of a low, flat, stomach-shaking explosion hit them. A puff of smoke climbed into the sky just around the turn in front of them.

"Shit!" Hunter said. He pulled his pistol.

When they came around the turn, they saw the three-quarter-ton chassis turned over on its side. The driver was lying nearby in a crumpled heap. There was a hole in the road where a mine had been detonated.

"Do you see anything?" Hunter asked.

"No," Ernie replied, sweeping his eyes along both sides of the road.

"There!" Hunter suddenly called. "Shit! We're dead even with them! I'm hauling ass!"

Ernie saw them as soon as Hunter called out. There were three of them. They looked like no more than teen-aged boys, the kind of pranksters who might stand on the side of the road and pelt cars with snowballs. But those weren't snowballs in their hands, they were AK-47's. And the mine they planted had already killed one man. This was no schoolboy prank.

Hunter pushed down on the accelerator and the Jeep shot forward. Ernie looked back and saw that the three V.C. had moved out in the open to start shooting. He could hear the bullets whipping by. One of them hit the left rear wheel well and clanged loudly as it poked through the skin of the Jeep.

"Shoot back at them!" Hunter called. "Make them duck!"

Ernie returned fire, the P-38 popping and bucking in his hand, kicking the spent shell casings away to glisten in the morning sun. He didn't hit anyone, but he did see a tree limb snap near the head of one, and that was enough to send the three of them scurrying for shelter. It was also enough to let them get out of range.

"Whooee!" Hunter said, laughing a few minutes later. "Wouldn't I have looked like an asshole if those little shits had got us, instead of the three-quarter?"

"If it had been us, I wouldn't be worried about looking like an asshole," Ernie said. He let the hammer back down on the pistol and moved the safety on.

"Yeah, but here I was using logic on that second lieutenant, explaining very carefully how the V.C. wouldn't attack just one Jeep, and that's exactly what they did do."

"Don't blame yourself," Ernie said. "I got a good look at them. They were even younger than the second lieutenant."

"Well, shit, no wonder," Hunter said. He took the pistol back from Ernie and put it in his pants-leg pocket again. "They probably don't know any more about what they're doing than that second lieutenant. Amateurs," he scoffed. "This whole fuckin' war's full of amateurs."

The next four hours were uneventful. The two men

ate C-rations for lunch. Ernie had ham and beans, Hunter chicken and noodles. At one of the little villages; they bought sliced fresh pineapple sticks rolled in hot peppers for dessert. It was three in the afternoon before they reached An Loi.

"Home, sweet home," Hunter grunted.

An Loi was a small, out-of-the-way security base. There was only one battalion of infantry at An Loi, so there was none of the order and plan of the larger bases. There were only three or four wooden structures here. The G.I.'s lived in G.P. medium tents with the sides rolled all the way up. Sandbags were stacked around each tent, forming a wall that rose halfway to the top. The tents, sandbags, and vehicles were covered by a layer of red dirt. There was a distinct smell to the place, a smell that was different from the larger bases. It was the smell of sweat, dirt, musty canvas, gun oil, and open-slit trenches.

Hunter parked in front of one of the tents.

"Home, sweet home," he said. "We can rustle up an extra bunk and mosquito net; you can come in with us if you want."

"That'll be fine," Ernie agreed.

A PFC came up to the Jeep. He was wearing dark-rimmed glasses and had a look about him that suggested he might be a clerk. The clerk looked over at Ernie, neither in welcome nor disdain, nor even with too much curiosity.

"McKay, this is Ernie Chapel," Hunter said. He's a newspaper reporter, come to do a story about us."

"That'll be nice," McKay said, almost distractedly. "Uh . . . Sergeant Two Bears . . . Colonel Petery wants to see you soon as you get back."

"Okay," Hunter said.

"He wants you to take over the platoon for Lieutenant Cox."

Hunter looked at him. "What happened to Cox?"

"Cox is the new company commander. Captain French was killed last night."

Hunter let out a slow breath. "Shit!" he said. "He only had six weeks to go, didn't he?"

"Less than that. He was down to twenty-nine days," McKay said.

Hunter nodded toward Ernie. "Get him some gear, set him up in my tent."

"Okay," McKay said. He motioned toward Ernie. "You gotta carry your own bunk, though. I only carry for officers."

"Lead on, McDuff," Ernie said jovially.

"It's McKay," the clerk said.

# Chapter Three

Colonel Petery's office was usually cold enough to hang meat. The Vietnamese house girls who worked there complained bitterly about having to clean his office, saying that it was like working in a freezer.

When Hunter went in this day, however, the colonel's office was as hot and muggy as anyplace else on the compound. There was no mystery to it; Hunter saw the problem at once. Colonel Petery's air conditioner was disassembled and spread out on his desk.

"Sergeant Hanlon got off okay, I take it?" Petery asked. Petery was working on his air conditioner and he picked up a small piece and blew on it, then held it up and looked at it.

"Yes, sir, no problem."

"Captain French got killed last night," Petery said.

"Yes, sir, that's what I heard. How did it happen?"

"He took the ambush patrol out. Trouble is, our ambush patrol was ambushed."

"By the Ghost Patrol?" Hunter asked. The Ghost Patrol was what the men of An Loi called a North Vietnamese Army unit that was operating in the area. The name came from the fact that the patrol would sneak in from Cambodia, raise hell, then slip back across the border before the Americans could react.

"Nobody else," Petery said.

Hunter ran his hand through his hair. "Shit! What was Captain French doing out there, anyway?"

"I told him he didn't have to take the patrol," Petery went on. "I told him that's what we've got lieutenants for." He looked up at Hunter. "And sergeants," he added. He sighed. "But, you know French. He believed company commanders should take their turn, just like everyone else."

"Any more casualties?"

"No. He was the only one." Petery was trying, unsuccessfully, to fit two pieces together. Hunter took them from him and, with one deft motion, had them connected. He handed them back. "Thanks," Petery said. "Sergeant, I'm not going to transfer another officer to the company. I want you to take over the platoon."

"Colonel, there are a couple of lieutenants back at headquarters chomping at the bit for some combat command time," Hunter reminded him.

"Yeah, well, let 'em learn somewhere else. I don't have time to make their Form-66's look good. I've got a damned job to do, and I intend to use the best people I have to do it. I have special plans for you. That's why I moved Cox up to take over the company."

"I wanted to ask you about that," Hunter said. "Lieutenant Donlevy has been in-country longer. Wouldn't it be better to give him the command?"

"It might be. But there's a reason to my madness. I told you, I wanted to get Cox out of the way so you could take the platoon. I want you to go after the Ghost Patrol."

"Yes, sir, I'll take an ambush patrol out tonight," Hunter offered.

"It's going to take much more than an ambush patrol," Petery said. He put down the pieces of the air conditioner, then walked over to a map and pointed to it. "In the past week alone, the Ghost Patrol have hit Phu Loi, Di An, Phuoc Bin, and Phu Cuong. Mr. Mot tells me that the locals are beginning to talk about them as if they were some kind of heroes. They're taking on the U.S. Army and they're kicking ass."

"Well, Colonel, so far they *have* kicked our ass," Hunter said.

"I know that, goddammit!" Petery said. "I know it, but I don't like it. Not only that, other people are starting to imitate them. Some of the local V.C. units that have been inactive for months are beginning to stir again because they're getting fired up by the Ghost Patrol. Hell, a V.C. sapper squad even hit Ton Son Nhut last night."

"I know, I was there," Hunter reminded him.

"Yes, so you were." Colonel Petery took a handkerchief from his pocket and wiped sweat from his face.

"Well, here's the problem, Sergeant Two Bears. We were put up here specifically to interdict these roving V.C. patrols, to keep them away from places like Phu Loi and Di An. Until this NVA outfit came down here, we were keeping things pretty well under control. Now it's all going to hell in a basket and USARV is on my ass wanting to know what the hell I'm doing about it."

"I see."

"No, Sergeant, I'm not sure you do see. I'm a lieutenant colonel in the zone for 0-6. I would really like to make 0-6 before I retire. And not just because I want to put a little bird on my collar. I plan to retire in a couple of years, and the difference in retirement between an 0-5 and an 0-6 is the difference between owning a thirty-five-foot cabin cruiser and a fourteen-foot bass boat. Do you get my drift?"

"Yes, sir."

"Good. Because this is what I want. I want you to take an augmented platoon out on a total sweep. Stay gone for a week if necessary . . . we'll arrange for resupply. I want you to find the Ghost Patrol and eliminate them."

"Did you say an augmented platoon, sir?"

"Yes. You can take some mortars from the weapons platoon, extra ammo from headquarters platoon. Whatever it takes to get the job done, you can have."

"Yes, sir," Hunter said.

"Do you have a problem with that?" Petery asked.

"I have no problem, Colonel, but you might," Hunter said. "You've got half a dozen officers in the battalion who are going to raise hell when they learn that an augmented platoon is going to the field with an NCO in charge."

"You let me worry about the officers' wounded feelings," Petery said. "You just take care of the job I gave you."

"Yes, sir."

"How soon can you be ready?"

"I'd like to assemble the platoon, take them out on a few ambush patrols and see how they work together. Give me, say, a week, and we'll be ready."

"Fine, fine. Oh, by the way, we got some steaks in this morning. Bet it's a long time since you had a good steak, hasn't it?"

Hunter thought of the steaks he had taken from the officers' grill last night. Until then it had been a couple of months since he saw one.

"Yes, sir," he said. "Quite a while."

"Last week I had to go to Saigon, as you know. I ate in the consolidated mess. They had steak. The straphangers had steak, while the guys in the field were eating C's. Well, I raised hell with food service and it paid off." Petery wiped his face again. "Wouldn't you know this son of a bitch would break down on the hottest day of the year?"

Hunter chuckled. "You keep it so cold in here that how would you know whether it's the hottest day or not?"

"Well, there you go, it's the hottest day for me," Petery said.

"Set it up there," McKay said, pointing to a spot on the plywood floor near the front of the tent.

With a grunt, Ernie set down the bunk, mattress, pillow, pillow cover, sheets, and two blankets. He pulled out the fold-up legs, then set up the bunk. He unrolled the cotton mattress, put on the sheets, slipped on the pillowcase, then made the bed with hospital corners, and was ready.

There were two men at the far end of the tent. One was in his underwear. The T-shirt was green, but the shorts were white. There was a pan of water on the top of the pile of sandbags and he was shaving, though being very careful to leave his moustache in place. The moustache was light-colored, bushy, with tips that twisted around the sides of his mouth. He looked to be about twenty.

One of the other men was sitting on a box, cleaning his rifle in a can of gasoline. The smell of gasoline was so strong that Ernie coughed. The rifle cleaner was bare from the waist up, though he was wearing fatigue trousers and jungle boots. He was also wearing a knife — not a bayonet, but a large Bowie knife.

"You the new platoon sergeant?" someone asked. The man who asked the question was about twenty-six. He was wearing an unbuttoned shirt with the sleeves rolled up, though his staff sergeant stripes could be seen.

"No," Ernie said. "I'm not in the army. I'm a newspaper reporter."

"I told you not to get all uptight, Mills," one of the other men said. "Mills is acting platoon sergeant now. He thought you were coming in to take his job away from him."

"Some job," someone said. "He's only had it for half a day."

"Far as I'm concerned, you still have it," Ernie said, smiling, and holding up his hands. "I don't want anything to do with it."

"No shit! You're a newspaper reporter, huh?" Sergeant Mills said. "What are you doing out here in the boonies with us? Seems like you'd want to stay in Saigon, where you know what's going on."

"The only thing you learn in Saigon is what acts are playing at what clubs," Ernie said.

"Ain't that the shits? I got a buddy in the 56th Trans Company. He's always writin' me about what he done the night before at the NCO club, or downtown, or out on Plantation Row."

"What's Plantation Row?" someone asked.

"Don't mind him, he's a fuckin' new guy," someone said. "Plantation Row is a street full of nothing' but bars and whorehouses. It's about two clicks down the road from the main gate at Ton Son Nhut."

"Shit! Those guys fight some kind of war, don't they?"

"Sergeant Mills?" someone called from the front of the tent.

"Yeah. What do you want, Evans?" Evans was in full uniform, including hat and polished boots. He had a fresh look about him, the look of one who spent all his time in an air-conditioned room.

He looked over at Ernie with an expression of curiosity on his face. Nobody volunteered any information.

"I been crankin' your phone for the last ten minutes. What's wrong with it?" Evans asked.

"Nothing's wrong with it," Mills said.

"The hell there's not. Look, there's the problem," Evans said, walking over toward the phone. "You've let your line come loose."

"Leave it alone!" Mills bellowed.

Evans looked at Mills and the others in frustration.

"Are you crazy? All you have to do is connect that line and your phone will work."

"I told you, there's nothing wrong with it. It's just the way we like it."

"Nobody from the orderly room can get you as long as it's like that."

"Yeah," Mills said, smiling. "We noticed."

"Well, maybe that's good for you," he said. "But that means I have to walk down here every time Lieutenant Cox wants to see you."

"You need the exercise," Mills said. He started buttoning his shirt. "What's he want?"

"I don't know. He just asked me to tell you he wanted to see you. I'm supposed to have a file on everybody that comes in. Who is this? I didn't even know he was here," Evans said, finally giving in to curiosity about Ernie.

"He's C.I.D.," Mills said. "You're not supposed to know he's here."

"Criminal Investigation Division?"

"Yep."

"What's he investigating?"

"There's a rumor that the guys in headquarters

platoon are all queer for each other," the soldier with the moustache said. "He's checking it out."

"I'm in headquarters platoon."

"I know — that's why you weren't supposed to know." Mills put his arm around Evans's shoulder. "We know you're okay; it's those other guys we're worried about. Don't tell anyone, okay?"

"Okay," Evans said. He looked over at Ernie. "I swear, I won't say a thing."

Ernie laid his finger across his lips and shook his head.

"I promise," Evans said as he and Mills started toward the orderly room to see Lieutenant Cox.

When Lieutenant Larry Cox was made company commander, he moved his bunk, wall, and footlocker into the orderly room. It was more lonely there than it had been in "The Grotto," as the officers called their tent. There were six lieutenants and two warrant officers in The Grotto, and they shared a refrigerator, bar, and two house girls. They didn't have an air conditioner, though, and the orderly room did. That provided some compensation for being alone.

Cox got his commission through the ROTC. Unlike many other ROTC officers, though, Cox had every intention of making the army his career. He planned to apply for a regular army commission as soon as this tour was completed.

His chances for getting an RA commission were enhanced, he thought, by the fact that he had been named company commander for a line infantry company, even though he was just a lieutenant. He had been very pleased with that appointment. When he learned that Colonel Petery planned to send a platoon, his old platoon, out after the Ghost Patrol, he immediately volunteered. He was surprised and frustrated when Petery turned him down.

A sergeant. The platoon was going out under the command of an NCO. How was that going to look on his records, if people realized that the battalion commander had so little faith in him that he sent a sergeant first class out in charge of an augmented platoon?

There was a knock on the door of the orderly room.

"Enter," Cox called.

Staff Sergeant Mills came in, then saluted. "You wanted to see me, sir?"

"Yes, Sergeant Mills," Cox said. Cox ran his hand across the top of his head. He did have hair, but he was very blond and he kept his hair cut so short that at first glance he looked bald. "Have a seat, Sergeant."

"Thank you, sir."

"Sergeant Mills, I've been talking to the colonel about you."

"About me, sir?"

"Well, about you and the entire platoon. You know it's a big job to act as platoon sergeant when there is no officer in the platoon."

"Yes, sir, I know. That's why I'm glad SFC Two Bears is here."

"Mills, I think — that is, the colonel and I think — that your platoon could handle a big assignment. We're sending you out after the Ghost

Patrol. There won't be any officers . . . You and Two Bears will have the whole thing to yourself. Do you think you can handle it?''

"Yes, sir,'' Mills said.

Cox smiled. "That's just what I told the colonel. He wasn't so sure, but I persuaded him to give it a try. You aren't going to let me down, are you?''

"No, sir. Uh . . . Lieutenant Cox, shouldn't Hunter be here?''

"Colonel Petery is briefing Sergeant Two Bears,'' Cox said. I asked to brief you personally. We have something in common, you and I. We're both filling positions of more responsibility than our rank calls for. I'm a platoon leader serving as company commander; you're a squad leader serving as platoon sergeant. Because of that, we have to stick together.''

"Yes, sir,'' Mills said, not quite sure where Cox was going with all this.

"Now, here's what I want you to do. If you think the platoon is getting into a situation that is . . . well, more difficult than you anticipated, I want you to get word back to me.''

"I'm not following you, sir.''

"Say Sergeant Two Bears attempts to follow a course of action that is . . . in your eyes . . . not the wisest course of action. I want you to send me a message, a coded message known only to the two of us, and I'll come as quickly as I can. Send the words 'Garry Owen.' That was Custer's regimental song. That'll be a good signal. Custer sure bit off more than he could chew.''

"Lieutenant Cox, if Sergeant Two Bears is in

command, I have no right to question his orders,'' Mills said. "If I called you in behind his back, that would be the same as sedition.''

"No, no, I'm not asking you to disobey any of Hunter's orders," Cox said. "All I'm saying is that I went out on a limb, way out on a limb, to talk Colonel Petery into using my old platoon. I have every confidence that you and Sergeant Two Bears can handle it. But I'm afraid that Two Bears may get himself in a situation that is more difficult than he suspected, and he'll have too much pride to call for help. All I'm asking for is that you help me give Two Bears all the support he needs. You do see that, don't you?"

"I . . . I guess so," Mills said.

"Good," Cox said. "And I suppose that it also goes without saying that this conversation would be better kept between us. If Two Bears knew we were looking out for him, he wouldn't like it much, and Two Bears is not the kind of man we want to have against us, is he?"

"No, sir," Mills said, smiling.

"You do agree that this is the best way to handle it, don't you? I mean, if I went directly to him and asked him to call me if he needed help, it would be an insult."

"Yes, sir, I guess it would."

Cox stood up then, and in so doing signaled Mills that the meeting was over.

"After all, I do have a vested interest in this operation," Cox said. "If you guys look good it makes me look good. Now, any problems with what we've discussed?"

"No, sir."

"I hope you don't have to call me, Sergeant Mills, but I'll feel better knowing we have something to fall back on. Good luck."

"Thank you, sir," Mills said. He saluted again, then left.

Cox walked over to his bunk and lay down with his hands folded behind his head. By giving Sergeant Mills the opportunity to call if things weren't going right, he was also giving him the *idea* to call. No subordinate ever agreed with everything his senior did. This would make Mills question every action, and the more he questioned, the more chance there was that he would be called. There was no way Colonel Petery could refuse to let him go to the field if his men called for help.

Shit! This just might work out all right after all.

# Chapter Four

Ernie asked Hunter if he could go along on the ambush patrol that night. Hunter told him he could if he would keep his ass out of everyone's way and try not to get it shot off.

"But you better get a little rest if you can," Hunter added. "The nights get pretty long out there."

Most of the others in the tent, learning that they would have ambush patrol that night, sacked out for a little sleep. Ernie was surprised at how quickly the others were able to drop off. Within moments the rhythmic breathing and soft snoring told him that everyone in the tent was asleep.

Everyone but him.

Ernie lay on the bunk listening to the filtered sounds of the base. A stream of water ran by just outside the fence, and several Vietnamese women were doing their laundry there. They weren't aware that any of the Americans could overhear them, and one of them was talking in the most intimate detail about her sister's appraisal of G.I.'s as sex partners. They were playing a radio. The music was a tuneless song: all flute, drum, and half-tone nasal sounds from the female vocalist who was singing about a lover killed in the war. Diplomatically, the song didn't identify whether her lover was ARVN or V.C. Helicopters whirled in and out of the landing pad. Finally, even Ernie was able to drop off to sleep.

"Okay, Mr. Chapel, roll out of the fart-sack," someone said. "We're going to eat now."

Ernie joined the others as they walked toward the mess tent. There was a long line waiting to eat, but when Ernie started toward the end, Pepper, the young man with the moustache, reached out and grabbed him.

"We get to buck the line," he said.

"I don't mind waiting."

"It's not 'cause you're a hotshot reporter or anything," Pepper said. "Everyone on ambush bucks the line."

"The guys in the line don't mind?"

Pepper made a little sound deep in his throat. It could have been a laugh.

"Think anyone in this line would trade places with us?"

"Lookie there," one of the men in the chow line said. "They got some civilian going on ambush with them."

"Yeah? Better him than me," someone else said.

Supper was steak, french fries, corn, and Kool-aid.

"You guys eat like this all the time?" Ernie teased.

Pepper held up the Kool-aid. "Just this," he said. "No matter where we go, we got Kool-aid."

After supper, Ernie went back to the tent to join the others as they prepared for the ambush. Their faces were blackened, their trousers legs were tied to keep from rustling, and they were given their instructions. Hunter handed Ernie an M-16. Ernie held his hands up, declining the weapon.

"Hunter, you know what I told you. I can't take a weapon."

"You going out there without a piece?" someone asked.

"I have to. That's the rules."

"Rules? Rules? What do you think — there's going to be some asshole running around out there with a striped shirt and a red flag? You're going to get a fifteen-yard penalty or something? No way, man. This is fuckin' for real."

"I still can't carry a weapon."

"Pepper," Hunter said with a sigh, "keep him with you."

"Okay. Come on, Mr. Chapel, you can stay with me."

"I don't want to be a problem."

"You won't be," Pepper said. "We get into a firefight, I'm going to be shooting from behind you."

The others in the tent laughed.

"Here," Pepper said, handing a little bottle of insect repellent to Ernie. "The dinks can smell this shit half a mile away, but if you get to slapping and scratching at mosquitoes they can spot you for a mile."

Ernie rubbed his hands, face, and neck with the stuff. It burned his skin and the smell made his eyes water.

A few minutes later everyone who was going on the ambush patrol was assembled. It was immediately obvious that this wasn't a routine ambush patrol — there were at least three times as many people as normally went out.

"Okay, men, listen up," Hunter said. He stood in front of the others, his face smeared with the anti-glare paint, and for a moment Ernie could almost see Hunter's great-grandfather half naked and painted, astride a war pony, with a long, feathered lance by his side. "As you can tell by looking around you, this is not the routine patrol. This is an augmented patrol. We're going to take ambush for the next four nights. . . ."

"The next four nights?" someone groaned.

"The next four nights," Hunter went on, silencing the protestor with an intense stare, "until we can work together as a team. When that time comes we're going after . . ."

"Son of a bitch! We're going after the Ghost Patrol!" someone said, figuring it out before Hunter could say the words.

"Is that right, Sarge?"

"That's right," Hunter said.

"All right!"

"Fuckin' A!"

"Kick some ass!"

"What officer's going with us?"

"None," Hunter said. "There's just going to be Mills and me."

"Fantastic!"

"Tonight will be no different from any other ambush that you've been on, except we'll have more people out. I just want to see how we all work together, that's all. Remember, if we get contact, shoot low. Everyone always tends to shoot too high. Shoot at their knees, you'll be hitting them in the chest."

The M.P.'s at the gate watched as the patrol walked through. One of them was a lieutenant, and he was counting them and making a note in a small notebook.

"There's a lot of people here, Sergeant. You planning on starting a war?" the lieutenant quipped.

"Hey, any of you M.P.'s got a couple hundred extra P's? I might get lucky and find a piece of ass out there, only I don't have any money," Pepper said.

"Remember, keep five to ten meters apart," Hunter hissed as they started across the rice paddies. They walked along the dike, moving so silently that the only thing Ernie could hear was his own breathing and the sound of his heart beating.

They walked for twenty minutes, all the way across the fields that were close to the base, then through a narrow strip of wood line, and finally to the near edge of another field. This field was about two hundred meters across, and on the other side of it was the edge of a very thick growth of trees. Ernie saw Hunter and Pepper coming back toward him.

"You two guys will have this spot," he said. "Take up a good position behind this berm and don't talk. Pepper, your field of fire goes from that tall tree there, on your left. See it?"

"Yes," Pepper said.

"To that clump of bushes on the right. Get a couple of sticks and put them up in the berm for firing stakes. Anybody comes, they'll be coming through those trees."

"Right," Pepper said.

Hunter moved off to the left at a crouch to set up the next member of the team. Pepper signaled for Ernie to get down. Then he put up his stakes and slid down behind the berm, alongside Ernie.

"What if we see someone out there?" Ernie whispered.

"I'll shoot his ass."

"Without finding out if he's V.C."

"Look, Mr. Chapel, this ain't no social engagement. If I see anything moving out there, I'm going to blow its ass away no matter what the fuck it is: water buffalo, VC, ammo-bearer, kid going to school, or the Pope. Far as I'm concerned, they're dead meat."

"I understand," Ernie said.

"We're going to be here till daylight, so you may as well get comfortable."

"Okay."

It was quiet. Ernie could hear sounds from way off. In the village, which was about five kilometers away, someone was playing a radio and he could hear it quite clearly. It sounded like the same song he had heard earlier in the afternoon, but then, as long as he had been over here, they all sounded alike.

Ernie didn't think he'd dozed off, but a sudden long burst of automatic-weapons fire made him jerk his head up, and he knew he had been asleep. He saw a stream of orange tracer rounds spewing out toward the wood line, then another stream of tracer rounds, this time green in color, coming back.

All along the berm the Americans began firing. A moment later a mortar flare burst high overhead and it floated down slowly under the parachute, lighting the entire field as bright as afternoon. That was when Ernie saw them. At least thirty Vietnamese were moving on line, across the field. They were all dressed in black pajamas and sandals, and they were running bent over, carrying AK-47's and assorted other weapons. They hit the ground when the flare popped.

The nearest one was no more than one hundred meters out, and Pepper squeezed off a long burst. Ernie watched the tracer rounds spew out the end of Pepper's weapon and saw them spattering into the ground all around the Viet, but didn't see any hits. Pepper raised his sights and the stream of tracer rounds from his rifle made a gentle curve all the way to the trees.

"Damn! Too high!" Pepper said. Pepper pulled the trigger again, but he was out of ammunition.

Ernie felt his stomach in his throat. Here he was, without a weapon, sitting in the middle of a battlefield, just observing. The V.C. were coming right at him and he was helpless. To make matters worse, the man who was supposed to protect him was out of ammunition.

"Load it!" Ernie said. He handed Pepper another magazine. "Here, put it in, put it in!"

The flare burned out then, and it seemed much darker than it was before. That was when Ernie realized he had kept both eyes open during the time of the flare, thus destroying his visual purple. It would take him a few minutes to get back his night vision.

Tracer rounds zipped back and forth between the berm and the middle of the field, and Ernie saw a line of green squirt right for him, looking like a brightly strung line of glowing beads. Fortunately, the V.C. shooting toward him was making the same mistake Pepper had made and was firing too high, because the rounds zinged and popped by overhead.

Pepper fired off another magazine and had just loaded a third when another flare popped overhead. Ernie started to close one of his eyes this time, but he was shocked to see a V.C. right in front of them, no more than ten meters away. The V.C. froze for an instant, and Pepper, in fear and surprise, opened up on him. He fired off the entire magazine in one burst. Ernie saw blood squirt from the V.C.'s chest, neck, and face as he fell face down.

"Son of a bitch!" Pepper shouted excitedly. "Son of a bitch! That motherfucker was right on top of us!"

The augmented platoon had brought mortars with them and they opened up then. The first salvo exploded in the tree line, but the mortar crews began walking the rounds back across the field until they were coming almost straight down. They burst so close that Ernie could feel the heat and shock effect, and he got down behind the berm and put his face in the mud and prayed. If a V.C. happened upon him now, the V.C. could have him, because he was concerned only with surviving the American mortar barrage.

The fire fight was over almost as quickly as it began, and Ernie lay there behind the berm, startled by the sudden silence.

"You okay, Mr. Chapel?" Pepper asked.

"Yeah," Ernie said. His heart was beating fast, and he was gasping for breath, almost as if he had run a mile. Each gasp of breath hurt his nostrils, for the air hung heavy with the smell of cordite from the gunpowder. A cloud of gunsmoke hung over the field for several minutes before it finally drifted away. Finally, Hunter came running down the line, bent over low behind the berm. He called out to Pepper before he came over to him.

"Pepper, it's me, Hunter."

"Come on," Pepper answered.

"You guys okay?"

"Yeah," Pepper said. "How'd we come out?"

"One wounded, one K.I.A. at the other end of the line," Hunter said. "Haven't checked down here yet." He continued on down the line. "Mac," Ernie heard him call in the darkness. "Mac, it's me, Hunter."

"Does it get this exciting on every ambush mission?" Ernie asked.

"No," Pepper said. "Wish I could tell you this was old hat with me, but the truth is, I was scared shitless."

"You were scared shitless," Ernie said. "I, on the other hand, nearly crapped in my pants. I guess we had both ends covered."

"Yeah," Pepper said, laughing. "Yeah, I guess we did."

"Pepper, it's me, coming back," Hunter said a moment later, reappearing in the darkness. "They got Mac. I moved Peterson in closer. Move your left parameter over another fifteen degrees."

"Gotcha," Pepper said.

"And keep a sharp eye and ear open. We don't want the sons of bitches getting around our flank."

"Okay."

"How'd Ernie make out?"

Pepper chuckled. "You shoulda seen him, Sarge. I had my own cheering section here. He was yelling and passing me ammunition."

"You did all right," Hunter said. "Lots of guys would've cut 'n' run if they got in a fire fight like this — especially if they had no weapon and nothing to keep them here."

"Yeah? Well, believe me, if there had been a place to run to when it started, I might've done it," Ernie said.

"Ain't it the truth?" Hunter said. "Stay awake now." Hunter disappeared into the dark again.

There was no problem with Ernie dozing off anymore that night. He was wide awake from that moment until the sun finally came up. He watched the sky grow lighter, the stars fade, and the shadows move away from the trees. He saw the mist settle on top of the trees for a while, then start to dissipate as the sun climbed higher. And he saw the bodies of the dead Vietnamese spread out across the field in front of them.

"Okay," Hunter said. "They're sending a shithook for the dinks. They're going to sling-load them out of here so we don't have to buy them. But they want a body count."

All up and down the berm the men of the platoon stood and began working out the kinks. Ernie looked over to the left. About twenty meters down the dike he saw Peterson standing over something, and he thought of Mac. Ernie walked down to Peterson. Mac was sprawled, face down, across the dike. A sticky pool of blood oozed out from under his head, and his hair was matted with blood.

"I looked at him," Peterson said quietly. "He caught a round right in the forehead. It must've been right at the first; he never even changed magazines. Look, there's no more'n five or six empty shell casings that I can see."

"I never heard anything," Ernie said.

"He died quiet," Peterson said. "It's better when they die quiet. But then, Mac always was a real considerate kid."

Ernie walked out into the field where the V.C. lay sprawled in various positions of death. The V.C. had been surprised by the strength of the ambush platoon. Expecting a patrol of only one-third the size, they mounted a major attack, hoping to score a significant victory. It backfired and nearly thirty of them lay dead.

"Look them over good before you touch them," Hunter cautioned. "They might have had time to booby-trap some of them. Bring any papers to me.''

''You got it, Sarge,'' someone answered.

The helicopter came in then, a large twin-engined, twin-rotored Chinook. It settled onto the field and half a dozen men jumped out, dragging a large cargo net with them. The V.C. bodies would be loaded onto the cargo net, then carried to their final destination in a sling load beneath the chopper.

Ernie walked back to look at the one who had gotten so close to him. He had already been rolled over on his back. His face was ashen-gray, almost blue in color. His eyes were open wide, a little bugged out, and they were a deep, deep brown. There was no light in the eyes, and though the flies hadn't reached him yet, there was a line of ants crawling in and out of his mouth.

There was no way of telling how old he was. He could have been anywhere from fifteen to twenty-five. Ernie had observed that Vietnamese were that way. Until the age of thirty-five, they always looked much younger. After thirty-five they looked much older.

The dead V.C. was wearing a T-shirt, and smiling up from the front of the T-shirt was the face of Mickey Mouse. That image stayed with Ernie for a long time . . . a dead V.C. in a Mickey Mouse T-shirt.

# Chapter Five

Bill Hanlon was at the reception center in Oakland Army Air Terminal, standing in line for an airline ticket to Paducah, Kentucky. He had three stripes on his sleeves, two rows of ribbons, and a Combat Infantry Badge over his left pocket, and a First Infantry Division patch on his right shoulder, indicating the unit with which he was in combat. He was a combat veteran and he was twenty years old.

"Where you goin', Sarge?" a spec-four asked.

"Paducah, Kentucky."

"I got a Greyhound bus ticket to Memphis. You can have it for ten bucks, save yourself a little money."

"Why are you sellin' it?"

"My brother's here with his car."

"I don't know, riding a bus that far sure doesn't sound like fun," Bill said.

"Hey, don't sweat it, man. There ain't nobody on the son of a bitch except other guys from 'Nam. Shit, man, it'll be a fuckin' party all the way."

"You're next," the man behind the counter said.

"Wait a minute, I'm trying to decide," Bill said.

"You're holding up the line, Sergeant. Now either tell me where you want to go, or get out of the line."

Bill looked at the civilian behind the counter, and he smiled. "Why don't I just tell you where to go?" he asked. He looked at the soldier who offered him the Greyhound ticket. "You just sold yourself a ticket," he said.

"The bus'll be loadin' at that door back there," the soldier said, handing the ticket to Bill. "Nobody on it but G.I.'s."

Bill took his duffel over to the pile of duffels by the door and looked outside, just as the bus rolled up. There were about thirty soldiers, marines, and airmen standing around, and they let out a cheer when the bus arrived. The bus stopped with a squeal of air brakes, and the driver got out, then smiled sheepishly.

"Okay, guys, let's go," he said.

Bill found a seat about halfway back on the right, next to the window. He could feel the throb of the bus engine and the thump of the duffel bags being thrown into the luggage bay beneath him. A specialist-fourth sat in the seat next to him. The spec-four was wearing a shoulder patch from the 101st.

"Fuck it!" the spec-four said.

"Yeah, really," Bill answered.

When the bus was loaded it pulled away from the terminal. Three blocks later it stopped in front of a liquor store and everyone on the bus streamed inside and began buying liquor. Bill went in with the spec-four. Several men started getting six-packs of beer from the shelves.

"We got it cold in the freezer," the man behind the counter said.

"Cold? Who the hell drinks beer cold?" someone asked.

Bill took a six-pack over and started to pay for it.

"From you, I gotta see an I.D.," the clerk said.

"I.D.?"

"Yeah. How old are you?"

"I'm very old," Bill said. "I never thought I would get this old."

"What are you talkin' about, I.D?" one of the other G.I.'s asked. "Are you shittin' us? Nobody asked to see I.D. when they sent us on the line."

"Listen, fellas, it's the law," the clerk said.

One gray-haired sergeant stepped up to the counter. He looked to be in his late forties or early fifties.

"What about me, friend? Do you want to see my I.D?"

"What? No, of course not. It's just that . . ."

"I'm buyin' everything," the sergeant said. "You tell me how much it costs, they'll give me the money, and I'll give it to you."

"That doesn't change anything," the clerk protested.

"Oh, yes, it does," the sergeant insisted. "It keeps us from wasting your goddamned building."

"Yeah!" one of the others said.

The clerk looked around nervously. "All right," he said. "Buy your stuff quickly and then get out of here, will you? I don't want the police coming around. They'll shut me down."

Someone brought a girl on board at Las Vegas. At first Bill thought one of the men had just picked her up and talked her into going with him. Then he learned that she was a whore who had talked the G.I. into taking her along. He was going to get ten percent of her action, and she went to everyone on the bus asking what she could do for them, and naming her price.

Bill and the spec-four with him turned her down, but the two guys across the aisle accepted her offer, and Bill could see their shadows and hear their noises as the bus rolled through the dark desert country of the great Southwest.

As soon as Bill was home he took down everything that was on the wall of his room: the college pennants, the autographed pictures of football players, the press coverage of his own high school football days . . . everything. His mother and dad were divorced and his dad had remarried and was in St. Louis working at McDonnell. His mother worked in the traffic department of the local television station.

Bill and his mother were eating dinner alone, though his mother had a sales conference that night.

"Just leave the dishes," she said. "I'll take care

of them later." She hugged Bill again. "Oh, Bill, it is so good to have you back home again. You just don't know how good."

"Mom, do you think I could just drop you off at the meeting and have the car?" Bill asked.

"Why do you want to do that, dear?"

"I thought I'd go out to a few of the places and bum around a bit, maybe see a few of the guys."

"Well . . . I . . ." His mother started to refuse. Then she saw the expression on her son's face. "Sure, Billy, You can just drop me off and I'll have someone bring me back home. But dear, please be careful."

"Yeah," Bill said. "Yeah, I'll be careful."

Bill went to the Blue Tornado, a drive-in named after the local high school football team. He saw Jim Freeman's candy-apple Ford parked there and he smiled. It could have been eighteen months ago. Nothing had changed. He was home again.

Simon and Garfunkel were on the juke when he went inside. The booths were crowded and the place was heavy with smoke, real tobacco, no grass.

"Hey, Bill!" someone called. "Come here." It was Freeman.

"Hi, Jim. I see you're still driving your Ford."

"Anybody wants that baby, they're going to have to come up with some heavy bread. So, hey, what are you doin' home from school? Semester break or what?"

"School?"

"Yeah, aren't you going to Murray State to play basketball or something?"

"No, not yet," Bill said.

"You're not? What have you been doing?"

"I was in the army. I just got discharged."

"You couldn't have been in the army for three years already."

"I volunteered for the draft. That was only two years. Then I got an early-out because I went to Vietnam."

"You been to Vietnam?"

"Yeah."

Two of the girls who were sitting in the booth with their friend Eddie looked at Bill. They were pretty girls, eighteen or nineteen, and Bill thought he would like to know them.

"You must be some kind of jerk," one of them said.

"What?" Bill asked in surprise.

"A real nerd," the other said.

"Why?" Bill was hurt by their remarks. "Why would you say that?"

"You let them send you to Vietnam."

"That place is definitely uncool," the other girl said.

"I really had no choice," Bill said.

"Sure you had a choice. You could have gone to Canada."

"You've seen the posters, haven't you?" one of the girls asked. She pushed her lips out, poutingly. "Girls say yes to boys who say no," she said, sexily.

"And no to turkeys who say yes," the other put in coldly.

"What was it like?" Jim asked.

"What? You mean Vietnam?"

"Yeah. Did you kill anyone?"

Bill looked at Eddie and the two girls and saw in

their eyes the same kind of morbid curiosity he always saw in the straphangers and clerks who would visit a battlefield after a fire fight. Walking through the dead bodies was as close as they ever got to combat.

Why the hell should he give them any pleasure?

"No, I was a librarian at the service club in Saigon," he said. "I never got into the field."

The light of interest left the girls' eyes.

"Yeah?" one of them said. "Well, you were a real jerkoff for letting them send you over there in the first place."

"Listen," Bill said as he stood up, "I gotta go. I got my mom's car."

"His mom's car," Jim snickered.

Bill peeled away angrily from the Blue Tornado, then went into a liquor store, where he grabbed a bottle of whiskey. The clerk was in the back of the store as Bill dropped a twenty-dollar bill on the counter, then started back for the door.

"Just a minute, I gotta see some I.D.," the clerk shouted, coming toward the front.

"I don't have time," Bill said. "Just keep the change."

"I need I.D.," the clerk shouted louder.

"Here's your I.D., buddy!" Bill replied, giving him the finger as he went out the door.

Bill took the bottle home with him, and he went into his room with the newly bared walls and lay on his bed and began drinking from the bottle.

The bed was too soft, so he moved onto the floor.

It was eleven o'clock on a Friday night. That meant noon Saturday in 'Nam. Last Saturday morning Bill was still in the company. He and Pepper had gone into town to eat noodle soup for lunch. They got laid that afternoon. Then there was a short-timer's party. Then Hunter took him to Ton Son Nhut. Now, here he was, lying on the floor in his room looking at walls that didn't mean anything to him anymore.

"Let me tell you, guys, this being-home-shit isn't all it's cracked up to be," Bill said, holding up the bottle in a lonesome toast in the night.

Bill broke from the key and went up to guard the shooter. He put his hands straight up, but the shooter arched a long, high shot and the ball swished through the net. The coach blew his whistle.

"No, no, no!" the coach said, coming over to stand by Bill and the black kid who just made the shot. Bill and the other kid were covered with a sheen of sweat, and Bill wiped the back of his hand across his forehead to keep the sweat out of his eyes.

"Hanlon, what the hell are you doing?" he asked. "You let him get that shot off."

"Coach, I had good position on him," Bill said. "He just put it over me."

"Goddammit! Don't you understand anything, Hanlon? You think this is some goddamned high-school or church-league game? This is college ball, and in college ball you do whatever is required to stop the shot."

"What if I foul?"

"Foul him. Knock him on his ass if you have to. I don't want to see him get the shot off," the coach said.

"Ain't no way that fool gonna stop me, Coach," the black kid said. "I got all the moves."

"Do it again," the coach said.

They set up again, and again the black kid got off the shot. This time when he came back down, he caught Bill in the eye with his elbow. Bill saw stars and went to one knee.

"Get up, Hanlon," the coach said. "Get up and get tough! I thought you were a tough Vietnam veteran. Now do it again."

The kid didn't get off a third shot. When he went up this time, all elbows and shoulders, Bill threw a forearm at him, catching him in the nose, mouth, and Adam's apple. The black kid went down, spitting teeth and choking on a smashed Adam's apple.

"Goddamn! What happened?" the coach shouted.

"Is that tough enough for you, Coach?" Bill said, starting off the court.

"Mister, I don't like your attitude. I think you better give me about fifty laps around the court."

"Blow it out your ass," Bill said without looking back.

"You're off the team!" the coach shouted, his voice breaking in anger. "You hear me? You're off the team!"

"No shit."

"Why do you want to go back to Vietnam?" the recruiting sergeant asked.

"I can't take this shit over here," Bill said. "I can't adjust."

The recruiting sergeant shook his head.

"No," he said. "You can't say that. That's no good. If the shrinks think you are having trouble adjusting, they'll certify you as unfit for service in Vietnam."

Bill laughed. "I'm fit for service in Vietnam," he said. "It's the States I'm having trouble with."

"No good. You have to come up with another reason."

"What if I said I had a Vietnamese girl pregnant and I wanted to get back to marry her?"

"They'd probably send you to Europe."

"Okay, you're the expert. You tell me how I can do it."

"Career," the recruiting sergeant said.

"Career?"

"Sign up for six years. The promotion is faster in 'Nam. The army understands career ambition."

"All right," Bill said. "Make out the papers. I say whatever I have to say. Just get me back to my old unit."

"You're as good as there," the sergeant said.

# Chapter Six

Ernie caught a helicopter flight back to Saigon on the day after the night ambush patrol. He thanked Hunter for the ride, and for the experience, and promised to bring a quart of Old Grand-dad with him next time he came.

When he jumped off the helicopter at Hotel Three in Ton Son Nhut, he saw Marty Burke standing near the front door of the operations office. Marty was a reporter for the Smith-Baker Syndicate. When he first met her, Ernie, like many other newsmen, thought it was a mistake to send a woman reporter into a war zone. Despite his apprehensions, Marty had proven herself a very capable journalist, and Ernie now had a grudging respect for her. More than that, he had an admiration for her. The fact that she was an exceptionally pretty woman didn't hurt either.

"Where've you been?" Marty asked, holding her hat down against the rotor blast as a helicopter took off.

"An Loi," Ernie said. "Where are you going?"

"Just got back from My Tho," Marty said. "I'm trying to get a ride downtown to the Caravelle."

"Mind if I look for one with you?"

"I don't mind at all," Marty said. She smiled. "But if we find only one seat, I get it."

"You're on."

"Excuse me," a tall, thin spec-five said. He was walking by with a handful of papers. "Did you folks say you're looking for a ride to the Caravelle?"

"Yes."

"I'm going to the Brinks — that's right across the street. If you don't mind riding in the back of a three-quarter, you're welcome to come along."

"Sure. I don't mind three-quarters. Three-quarters are nice," Ernie said. "What about it, Marty?"

"Fine with me."

The two reporters followed the spec-five around the corner of the building to the parking area. Ernie climbed in first, then stretched a hand down over the tail gate to help Marty up. He put down the little bench seat along the side and they were ready to go.

Two Phantom Jets took off then and the noise of their engines rolled across the field like the roar of one hundred freight trains. Ernie could see them through the opening at the rear of the truck, and as soon as they broke ground they kicked in their afterburners and pulled back into a climb, riding atop twin pillars of fire, rocketing almost straight up until they were little more than bright dots high in the sky. In half an hour they would be over targets in North Vietnam. A bright green Braniff 707 started down the runway after the two Phantoms. On board were over two hundred returning servicemen finishing their tour. An Air Vietnam DC-6 turned onto the runway and Ernie could hear the sound of its four engines, whisper-quiet compared to the Phantoms, which could still be heard as a distant, rolling thunder.

The truck pulled away and they rode quietly for some time. Ernie looked through the back of the truck at the shade trees and white walls of Cong Ly as the broad street reeled out behind them. They passed bicycles, taxis, cyclos, Lambrettas, and other military traffic as the driver sped down the road, using his horn more often than the brakes.

Ernie couldn't stop thinking about the young V.C. in his Mickey Mouse T-shirt. When one thought of the godless, bloodthirsty commies, a teen-aged boy in a Mickey Mouse T-shirt was hardly the image that came to mind.

"Ernie?"

Ernie looked around and saw that they were stopped. It was then that he realized Marty was speaking to him, and had been.

"Oh, I'm sorry," he said. He let down the tail gate. "I guess I wasn't paying any attention."

"You didn't say a word all the way down here. Your mind was a thousand miles away," she said.

"No." He hopped down, then held her hand as she jumped from the back of the truck. "More like one hundred miles away."

"Want to talk about it over dinner?" Marty invited.

Ernie smiled. "No way would I waste the chance to have dinner with the lovely Marty Burke by talking business. We'll have dinner, but it's going to be purely social."

"Why, Ernie Chapel, are you asking me for a date?" Marty teased.

Ernie pulled himself up to full height and smoothed the jungle fatigues as well as he could.

"You're damned right I am," he said.

Captain Duong Cao Minh lay under the mosquito netting and tried to rest. There was practically no air moving, and what breeze there was; was stopped by the close weave of the netting. It was stiflingly hot, but at least he was under a roof and thus away from the sun. Many of his men were lying in the sun, or at best under the sparse shade of banyan trees.

His company had been badly cut up last night. He had expected to find no more than ten or twelve Americans out on their ambush patrol. Instead, he ran into a hornet's nest. There must have been thirty or more Americans out there, waiting for him. As a result of the battle, he lost over forty men.

"Are you awake?" the girl asked in a soft, melodic voice.

Minh turned his head and saw her standing by his sleeping mat. She was wearing freshly laundered clothing and her skin was clean and sweet-smelling. He knew she had done it for him and he was pleased. Being the commander of the largest People's Army Force unit in the sector did have its compensations.

"I want something to drink," Minh said. He sat up and pushed the mosquito netting to one side, then swung his legs out. They were muscular and dark and laced with the scars of a thousand grass cuts and insect bites, the souvenirs of years in the jungle. Minh could deny being V.C. all he wanted, but the moment they saw his legs they would know.

The girl nodded and rushed off. A moment later she returned and handed him a glass of cool, sweetened coconut milk. She smiled as if she were proud of her offering and he nodded at her and took it. He would have preferred something a little harder, whiskey if possible. At least a bottle of beer. But, what the girl lacked in perceptiveness, she compensated for in other things. He felt a warming of his blood as he recalled the sex they had had last night before his mission. He would have her again, tonight. Minh took the glass with a nod of thanks.

Minh finished the drink quickly, then stood up and walked outside into the streets of the little village of My Song. It was a small hamlet, with barely three dozen buildings. It had a store and a doctor's office, not a medical doctor, but a "folk doctor" whose remedies and potions were much preferred to a medical doctor's treatment. Two of the houses also doubled as cafés, and one of them kept whiskey and beer on hand.

As Minh walked through the dirt street of My

Song, there was very little about him to differentiate him from the other residents of the village. He wore nondescript clothing, and he was about the same size, though perhaps a little more muscular. His hair was black, his eyes dark brown, his skin darkened by the sun. His legs, with their mark of the jungle, were different, of course. He also wore a sidearm, a Chinese 9-mm pistol. That pistol was not only his badge, but also his guarantee of authority.

There were several reasons why Minh had chosen the village of My Song as his base of operations. It was centrally located to allow him to strike at many government targets. Americans never came to the village, and the government soldiers who did came by accident. The Saigon government did not consider My Song an important enough village to protect. Also, the sympathies of the village were generally with the V.C., and many of Minh's soldiers were from My Song.

As commanding officer of the V.C. company, Minh was accorded a status on par with that of the mayor and elders. In fact, Minh's soldiers did act as police for the village, so most regarded Minh not as a revolutionary, but as one of the establishment. They bowed, or looked away in respect, as he walked among them. He saw Sergeant Phat drinking beer at the little bar in the center of the village, and he joined him.

"Are the men resting well?" Minh asked. He pointed to a bottle of whiskey, and the proprietor, a little old man with a wispy white beard, poured him a glass.

"Some are resting better than the others, Captain," Phat said. "Mot's wounds are giving him much trouble."

"Will he survive them?"

Phat turned up the bottle of beer and took several long swallows, finishing it off. He let out a sigh of contentment and wiped his mouth with the back of his hand, then set the bottle down.

"I think he will die," Phat said. "I think he will die tonight."

"The ambush last night was costly," Minh said.

"Who would know that the Americans would have such a large patrol out?"

"It's because of our 'friends' from the north," Minh said, twisting the word "friends" so that it dripped with sarcasm. "Major Ngyuet takes his Ghost Patrol to the weakest point, scores a victory, and the Americans react as if they had been invaded."

"Major Ngyuet gets all the credit for our successes," Phat said.

Minh sighed. "For the moment that is good. The Ghost Patrol can keep the Americans occupied while we can move more freely. But, in the future, we must be certain of our targets. I have no wish to attack a force as large as the one we encountered last night, unless we are adequately prepared for it."

"We will have no such problems tonight," Phat said. "The target is an American communications station. There are only fifteen American soldiers there."

"You are certain of your information?"

Phat smiled. "I'm very certain. I have been inside the base every day for two weeks. I am the houseboy for the NCO hooch."

"Well, then we shall bring them a special delivery of laundry tonight, won't we?" Minh said.

The first time Ernie had sex with Marty, six months ago, he had felt almost incestuous. She was a reporter, a colleague, and in addition to being a fellow journalist, they had become great friends. He made that observation as they were dressing afterward.

"Don't feel bad," Marty had said. She leaned over to kiss him as she was buttoning her fatigue shirt across breasts Ernie had nestled his head against just moments earlier. "After all, what are friends for?"

As a result of that, they now had a password, known only to them, and used by them when one or the other felt the need. Marty was very open about her sexuality and sometimes initiated the action, as she had tonight, right after dinner, when she reached her hand across the table and asked Ernie if he would invite her to his apartment.

"Sure," he said, smiling. "After all, what are friends for?"

It was raining by the time they stepped out onto the street in front of the Caravelle, but there were always dozens of taxis hanging around the front of the hotel, so Ernie had no trouble getting one. He and Marty squeezed into the backseat of the little blue-and-yellow Renault.

"One fifty-three Le Loi," Ernie said.

As the taxi pulled out into the rain-slick street,

Marty slid her hand over to Ernie's and squeezed it. He looked at her and was surprised to see tears in the corners of her eyes.

"What's wrong?"

Marty shook her head in silence. Then she drew a breath. "I had a rough one this time out, Ernie," she said. She wiped her eyes with the back of her other hand and sniffed. "I know, I'm a reporter, I'm supposed to hold myself outside these things. But I had a man." She sighed. "No, he was a boy, just a boy, and he died in my arms. He was telling me how he scored the winning touchdown in their homecoming game last year, and how he had a date with the head cheerleader after the game." She laughed a weak, little laugh. "I learned later that he had actually sat on the bench for the whole game and his date was a French horn player in the band. But if it made him feel good to tell me, who was I . . . who was I to . . ." Her voice broke.

Ernie raised her hand to his lips and kissed it.

"So you can see why I wanted you to be my friend tonight," she went on. "I need to do something to put that out of my mind."

"I'll make us a pitcher of martinis," Ernie offered. "A couple of my martinis will put anything out of your mind," he teased.

"Oh, let's do, Ernie. Let's drink martinis and look at the rain and fuck like rabbits. I don't want there to be a thing in the world tonight but us . . . just us. No strain, no pain, just us."

Ernie's apartment was over a restaurant, reached by stairs that opened right onto the street. He had an open patio, furnished by rain-resistant furniture, and a bar under a small roof out on the patio. He stood under the roof mixing the martinis while the rain beat down on the blue-tile floor. Just behind him the door was open to his apartment, and in the apartment Marty was getting undressed.

Ernie carried the pitcher of martinis and two glasses back into the apartment, then saw Marty standing there waiting for him. Her breasts were small, firm, well rounded, and tipped by red nipples drawn tight by their exposure to the air. Her body was subtly lighted by the rain-dimmed light. The area at the junction of her legs was darkened by the shadows and by a tangle of dark hair that curled invitingly at her thighs.

Ernie poured two drinks and gave one to her, then set his down while he began taking off his own clothes. Marty drank hers, then, growing impatient, came over to help Ernie undress.

"I'll get your boots and trousers," she said. "You finish your drink."

By now, Ernie was as impatient as Marty, and when he was fully undressed he pulled her to him, kissing her open mouth with his own, feeling her tongue darting against his. He moved her toward the bed, then climbed in after her and crawled on top of her.

Marty received him happily, wrapping her legs around him, meeting his lunges by pushing against him. He lost himself in the pleasure of the moment, until a few minutes later she began a frenzied moaning and jerking beneath him. He let himself go then, thrusting against her, spraying his seed into her until finally he collapsed across her.

They lay together for a long time after that, lying

in the shadows of the room holding each other but not speaking. The shutters were still open and it was still raining, and the rain made music. For a long time the rain and their own afterglow cushioned them against all outside intrusion.

Then, little things began to creep in: the whir of motorbikes, the honking of horns, the clack of a soup vendor's sticks, the drone of a helicopter. The spell was broken and they weren't alone anymore. Ernie felt Marty crying on his shoulder and he pulled her to him and rubbed her hair and wished he could do or be whatever it took to make her hurt go away.

# Chapter Seven

Hunter could feel the sweat rolling down beneath his armpits, pooling in the small of his back, soaking through his shirt and causing it to stick to the tree he was sitting against. It was just before dawn and Hunter had taken his men out on the most ambitious project yet. This was to be a three-day mission to see what logistic problems the augmented platoon might encounter when they went on the big sweep.

In the strictest sense, this wasn't an ambush patrol since they didn't set up along one of the paths usually followed by the V.C. Because it wasn't an ambush party as such, Hunter had allowed the men to sleep last night, one-third awake, two-thirds asleep. That way, in theory at least, everyone got to sleep for two-thirds of the night. That was the theory . . . but Hunter had been awake for most of the night. He was disgusted with himself for not being able to sleep. It would make it twice as difficult for him to stay awake tonight. He rubbed his eyes and stared through the gloom.

What was the old saying? It was always darkest just before the dawn? Hunter could attest to that, at least here in Vietnam. He had made that very observation about hundreds of Vietnam dawns. The fact that they were in the jungle made it even darker, for whatever false dawn there may have been was blacked out by the trees.

He waited another thirty minutes.

From somewhere close by a monkey screeched. A frog began his morning song, and the birds awakened. The nocturnal insects grew dormant and the daytime insects started their activity as finally, through the trees, the sky began to lighten. A thin mist rose from the marshes and hung low over the jungle floor.

When it grew light enough for Hunter to move around without stumbling over things, he checked his men. There were no cherries in the platoon; every man had been on at least half a dozen patrols before. In addition, this was the fourth time out for the augmented platoon, which the men were now calling R&P for "Rape and Pillage." As a result, each of the men had taken up good positions of concealment, blending with the trees and grass so that unless one knew where they were, they could easily be overlooked.

"Good morning, Sarge," Sergeant Mills said.

"Did you get any sleep?" Hunter asked.

Mills grinned sheepishly. "No, not really," he said.

"Did you hear anything?"

"Not at thing. You?"

"About three o'clock this morning I heard two or three people walking. I didn't hear any conversation so I figure they were probably V.C., but it was such a small party it wasn't worth compromising our position."

"What do we do next?"

"Eat breakfast, no fires. Then we move out. Pass the word."

"Right," Mills said.

"Who we got carrying the radio? Goren?"

"Yeah."

"Goren, where are you?"

"Right here, Sarge," Goren answered, raising up from his spot. Goren was a small man with curly black hair and dark, horn-rimmed glasses.

"You got the day's push out of the S.O.I.?"

"Already have it cranked in."

"See if you can reach any air."

"Okay."

Goren moved out to a small clearing, raised his antenna, then began transmitting.

"Any air, any air, this is Wide Receiver, over."

Hunter looked through his C-rations until he found a can of ham and eggs. He hated the tinned ham and eggs at any time, but if he had to eat it, he'd rather try it for breakfast than be stuck with it for a lunch or supper meal. He took off his dog tag chain and, holding the small P-38 can opener between his thumb and forefinger, opened the can.

The pale yellow eggs and the gray chunks of ham were a sickening-looking, congealed mess. He opened the packet of pepper and dumped it in, then took a bite. He made a face as he forced it down.

"Any air, any air, this is Wide Receiver, over," Goren was saying, over and over in the background.

Mills came over and sat down beside Hunter. Mills was eating the bread roll and jelly and drinking tepid coffee from his canteen cup.

"What are we going to do today?" Mills asked.

"I thought we'd go west another twenty clicks. If we don't find anything we'll bivouac for the night and start back to An Loi tomorrow morning."

"Go west twenty clicks?"

"Yeah."

"Any air, any air, this is Wide Receiver, over."

"Damn! Sarge, twenty clicks west will put us in Cambodia," Mills observed.

"We won't cross over," Hunter said. "But if we can find where Charlie crosses, we might set up a toll booth."

"Roger, Army 775, this is Wide Receiver. Wait one. Sarge, I got somebody," Goren called.

Hunter put down his can of ham and eggs, three-quarters eaten now, brushed his hands together, then took the hand receiver from Goren. "Army 775," Goren whispered.

"Army 775, this is Wide Receiver 6," Hunter said. That was an exaggeration. Six meant commanding officer. Hunter was in charge, but technically he wasn't in command, since command was the exclusive right of commissioned officers. But Hunter reasoned that if the pilot of Army 775 felt he was talking to a commanding officer, he would be more responsive.

"This is Army 775." Hunter could hear the sound of the aircraft engine in the background.

"Army 775, we are at Tango Papa 4140. We want your eyes. Are you in the vicinity?"

"Two minutes out," Army 775 answered.

"Army 775, in two minutes I'll pop smoke. I'd appreciate it if you'd take a look around then and see what's going on."

"Roger, 775 out."

"Mills," Hunter said, "bring a can of smoke."

Sergeant Mills picked up a smoke grenade, then walked over to stand by Hunter. It was a gray canister, about the size of a beer can, with a yellow band around the top.

"I see him, Sarge," Goren pointed out.

By now Hunter could hear him. It was a Huey, skating low and fast over the trees, the angry snarl of his engine rolling out before him.

"Now, Mills."

Mills pulled the pin on the smoke grenade and rolled it away from them. A billowing gush of dark yellow smoke spewed from the canister, then climbed up into a lighter yellow column that rose above the trees.

"Wide Receiver, I roger yellow smoke."

"That's affirmative."

The Huey zipped by overhead, then climbed and made a wide circle to the north.

"You've got a large, open area about two clicks

to your west," the pilot said. "Some huts at the north end of the open area. I don't see any people."

"Army 775, are there any animals by the huts?"

"Animals?"

"Goats, sheep, water buffalo — anything like that."

"I'll go down and take a look."

"What you want to know about animals for, Sarge?" Mills asked.

"If there are any there, it might really be a farmer's hooch. Otherwise, it could be V.C.," Hunter explained.

"Wide Receiver, negative on the animals," the pilot said.

"Thanks, Army 775. Wide Receiver out."

Minh was west of the open field when the helicopter passed over the first time. He was coming back from a raid on the American commo post. It had been successful. He hadn't actually breached the perimeter, but he had destroyed the generator and transmitter and he was sure he had inflicted heavy casualties against the Americans. He had lost only two men.

When the helicopter passed overhead a moment earlier his first thought was that the Americans had followed them from the transmitter and were going to launch a helicopter attack. Then, when he saw that this wasn't a gunship and there were no other helicopters nearby, he knew that wasn't it.

"Shall we shoot him down, Captain?" Phat asked.

"Yes," Minh replied. He smiled. "It will be a good finish to our night's work."

Phat called to the men and half a dozen moved into position. They fit the special sighting devices onto the ends of their weapons, devices that deflected the sight and gave the proper lead necessary to bring down a helicopter flying at seventy-five knots.

"Wait!" Minh called suddenly. The men looked over toward him in surprise.

"What is it, Captain?"

"Look, on the other side of the field. There is yellow smoke. There are Americans over there."

"Hold your fire!" Phat said to his men, waving with his hand to cause them to lower their weapons.

"If we shoot down the helicopter now we will expose our position," Minh said. "Get the men spread out and concealed."

Phat gave the necessary order and the little brown men disappeared into the trees.

"What do you think it is?"

"I don't know," Minh replied. "But if it's no larger than company strength, we can wipe them out." Minh smiled. "Now, we repay the Americans for the disaster of the other night."

Minh lay in position behind a log and raised his glasses to his eyes, searching the wood line on the other side of the clearing. He would open fire when they were totally committed to the open area, but before they were halfway. That way there would be some doubt in the minds of the Americans as to which way they should go. It would be very difficult for them to continue across the open field in the face of fire, especially if they had no idea of the size of the force they were facing. On the other hand, the natural tendency of the commander would be not to allow his men to retreat. That would keep the Americans in the killing zone for some time.

Hunter had his men at the tree line, looking across the clearing. The pilot had seen nothing during his recon, but that didn't really mean anything. And the fact that there were no animals around the huts bothered him. Still, he couldn't stay here all day.

"What do you think?" Mills asked.

"We can't stand around with our thumb in our ass," Hunter said. "Let's get across the son of a bitch. Keep the men on line, and keep them spread out," he said.

Hunter started his platoon across the field. The men, carrying their weapons at high port in front of them, jogged across the open ground. Except for the sound of breathing and the jiggle of equipment, there was absolute silence — as though time had stopped.

Hunter heard the sound of the mortar rounds leaving the tube, then the crash of their explosions in the middle of the field. That was followed immediately by the rattle of machine guns. Smoke began to drift out of the trees across the field and Hunter saw the winks of light as dozens of automatic weapons fired at them.

Hunter dived to the ground, then cut loose with a long burst from his M-16. "Get down!" he shouted. "Return fire!"

All up and down the line the Americans hit the ground within seconds tracer rounds were zipping across the field into the trees.

The V.C. mortars were continually firing and Hunter had the sickening sensation of seeing the bloody stump of a man's arm land in front of him. The watch was on the wrist, a ring on the finger. The hand was moving slightly, though the arm was totally severed. Hunter heard someone screaming for a medic.

"Oh, God! I'm hit! I'm hit!" someone screamed. Hunter saw a man get up and start running. He was holding his hands over his stomach, trying to keep a large loop of intestine from spilling out.

"Get down!" Hunter called. "Get down!" Hunter got up and ran toward the wounded man, then knocked him down.

"My gut's on fire, Sarge," the man said.

The V.C. were raking the area with machine gun and mortar fire. For the Americans it was like being caught in a meat grinder.

"We've got to get back to the tree line," Hunter told Mills. He made a motion toward the tree line. "Every other man, fall back!" he called. It was a procedure they had practiced and it allowed an orderly retreat. Half the men got up and started back, some of them dragging, helping, or carrying wounded buddies. The other half stayed on line to provide covering fire. When the first group reached the trees they would provide covering fire while the rest withdrew.

Hunter looked at the wounded soldier. He didn't know if it would be better to throw him over his shoulder or drag him. Either way was going to make the wound worse, but at least if he dragged him the wounded man wouldn't be as good a target. He grabbed the man by the ankles and started to pull.

It was at least thirty yards back to the tree line. Hunter could feel and hear the bullets all around him as he ran back, but none of them hit him. When he finally got there he pulled the wounded man over a little rise to get him out of the line of fire. Hunter looked back the way he had come and saw a trail of blood on the ground, marking their path. He felt weak and he looked at the wounded man to apologize. The man was unconscious.

"Sarge!" Goren called. "Sarge, I got the air force! They can get a couple of Phantoms here!"

"Call them in!" Hunter said.

"They want you to pop smoke!"

Hunter pulled a smoke canister from his pack, then tossed it into the open field. Green smoke began billowing up.

"Tell them to raise hell with the west side of the open field where the smoke is!" Hunter shouted.

Less than thirty seconds later it sounded like the whole world opened up. Two F4-C's screamed over just above the treetops. One was firing cannon and machine guns, the other rockets. Hunter could see explosions ripping through the trees on the other side.

"Napalm!" he shouted. "I want them to barbecue their ass!"

Both jets were pulling up from their strafing run, probably three miles beyond their target. They were climbing straight up, leaving a trail of black smoke behind them. Hunter ran over to get the radio.

"Fireman, this is Wide Receiver 6. Burn them out!"

"We're not carrying napalm," Hunter heard one of the pilots answer. He could tell from the pilot's voice that he was feeling the G's of the pull-up. By now the planes were tiny dots, high in the sky. "We've got enough ordnance to make it pretty uncomfortable for them, though. Keep your heads down. We're going to swing around for another run."

Hunter watched the jets peel off, then hurtle down from the sky so that in a matter of seconds they were no longer distant dots, but once again awesome war machines spitting fire and death into the tree line across the field. There were more explosions across the way and half a dozen trees were knocked down by the heavy machine gun and cannon fire. Both jets kicked on their afterburners for their climbout, and the noise that rolled across the field was so intense as to almost stun the senses.

After two more passes the Phantoms left and Hunter and ten men advanced across the field to where the V.C. had been. When they got there they found three V.C. bodies, but nothing else. He hurried back across the field to check on his casualties.

"Call in Dustoff," he said. "The area's clear."

# Chapter Eight

Ernie stood just inside the gate and watched as Hunter brought the R&P platoon back in. The men were tired and dirty and they stared straight ahead with what infantrymen called the "thousand-yard stare." Ernie had already heard about the fire fight they'd had yesterday morning. Four men were taken out by Dustoff. All four were in the First Field Hospital in Saigon. The spec-four with the traumatic amputation of his arm and the spec-five with the gut wound would be heading for the 106th General Army Hospital in Yokohama, Japan. The other two, whose wounds were less severe, would stay in-country.

Hunter saw Ernie and stepped away from the others to stand beside him. "Did you bring it?" he asked.

"Yes." Ernie knew he was asking about the Old Grand-dad.

"In my tent, soon as I finish debriefing the colonel."

"I'll be there," Ernie said.

The men of the R&P platoon were dismissed. Ernie watched them as they broke up. Some went immediately to clean their weapons, some started toward the shower, not even bothering to stop by their tents for clean clothes. Some went right to their bunks and fell across them with weapons, helmets, and web gear still attached.

Hunter went to Colonel Petery's hooch.

"What happened?" Colonel Petery asked. Hunter noticed that the colonel had evidently given up on fixing his old air conditioner. A newer, bigger model sat in the window, pumping out frigid air. It was so cold in Petery's office that fog came from his mouth when he spoke. Hunter tried to find a position to be out of the icy blast.

"We made our first contact yesterday morning," Hunter said.

"NVA?"

"No, sir, V.C.," Hunter said. "At least, the bodies we found were V.C."

"How many bodies?"

"We found three," Hunter said. "If there were any more, they were taken away. And, of course, we have no idea of how many may have been wounded."

"No matter, you gave a good accounting for yourselves. We know they had three K.I.A.; you didn't have any."

"I don't know if we can take credit for the K.I.A. or not," Hunter said. "We called in an air strike and they laid some pretty heavy ordnance onto Charley."

"You were on the ground — they're your body counts," Petery said. "You sure they were V.C. and not the NVA Ghost Patrol?"

"They were V.C., Colonel."

"Damn. I was hoping we made contact with the Ghost Patrol. How big was the unit?"

"From the firing pattern I'd say there were fifty or more."

"That big, huh?"

"At least that big, Colonel. Maybe more."

Colonel Petery rubbed his chin with his hand and leaned back in his chair.

"My guess is it's the same group that hit Tac Alpha. That's the remote commo unit that was hit night before last. They lost their transmitter and had two K.I.A."

"American K.I.A.?"

"Yes."

"Damn!" Hunter said.

"It all goes back to the Ghost Patrol," Petery said. "I'm telling you, until we wipe out the Ghost Patrol, every disgruntled dink in the sector is going to pick up a rifle and come after us."

"Begging your pardon, Colonel, I don't think the Ghost Patrol has any effect at all on these guys. They were tough, disciplined, well led, hardcore V.C. Would you like my opinion?"

"Why not?" Colonel Petery answered. "Opinions are like assholes. Everybody has one."

"I think we should forget about the Ghost

Patrol. These guys we ran into yesterday are the ones we want to go after. They're a hell of a lot more dangerous than the Ghost Patrol, because this is their home territory. They're going to be here after the Ghost Patrol has left.''

"We're going after the Ghost Patrol," Petery said. He leaned forward and put both hands on his desk. "Mind now, Sergeant Two Bears, I'm not saying there's no validity to what you're proposing. These guys probably are the real power in this sector. But the Ghost Patrol is beginning to build a reputation for themselves, and I don't like that. I particularly don't like it that they are doing it at my expense. Take care of the Ghost Patrol. Then we'll go after the people who hit you yesterday morning.''

"Yes, sir," Hunter said.

"Now, suppose you and your men take a twenty-four-hour standdown," Petery suggested.

"Thanks, Colonel. They'll appreciate it.''

There was laughter from the shower as Hunter approached it. "It's *my* dick. I'll wash it as fast as I want," someone said.

Hunter hung his towel on a nail and laid his kit on the wooden bench. He had stripped to his O.D. boxer shorts for the walk to the shower, and the only article of clothing he brought with him was a change of undershorts.

Some of the horseplay stopped when he stepped under the shower. It was as if an officer had arrived. The men didn't salute him, or say "sir" to him or anything, but they treated him with the same deference as they would an officer. At first Hunter had been puzzled by it. Then he realized that in his current position he had more direct influence over them than any other human being. Never mind President Nixon, General Westmoreland, or General Abrahams; when it came down to the nut-cutting, it was Sergeant First Class Hunter Two Bears who made the life-and-death decisions for them. Hunter nodded at the others, then stood over under the end nozzle, alone.

Ernie Chapel was standing just outside Hunter's tent, leaning against the half wall of sandbags, when Hunter came back, his Ho Chi Minh sandals flopping with every step. Hunter didn't say a word. He just stuck his hand out and curled his fingers in an expression of "give me." Ernie put the bottle of whiskey in his hand.

Hunter held up the bottle, letting the golden fluid capture a sunbeam, then shoot it back as if the bottle contained liquid fire. He unscrewed the cap, passed it under his nose, then turned it up and drank several Adam's apple-bobbing swallows. When he brought the bottle back down it was clear for the entire neck and down about half an inch below the shoulder of the bottle.

"Damn!" Ernie said. "I thought you Indians couldn't handle firewater."

Hunter wiped the back of his hand across his mouth, then let out a loud, satisfied belch.

"That was a myth the white men put out," he said. "They were afraid we'd drink it all and they couldn't have any." He passed the bottle over to Ernie. "Just to show you they were wrong, you can have a snort."

"Thanks," Ernie said. He turned it up and took a couple of swallows, then handed it back.

"I guess you heard I got some men shot up yesterday?" Hunter asked.

"Yeah. I checked in the hospital before I came up here. Meagher and Billings are fine."

"What about Poindexter and Spears?"

"I wish I could tell you something about them," Ernie said. "All I heard was that they are stable."

"Stable? What the hell does that mean?" Hunter asked. "Dead people are stable, aren't they?" Hunter took another swallow of his whiskey. "What's green and red and going a hundred miles an hour?" he asked.

"I don't know. I give up," Ernie said.

"A frog in a food blender." Hunter belched.

Ernie chuckled. "Gross, Hunter. That was gross."

"That's what it was like, Ernie. We were frogs in a food blender. Shit! I led them right into it."

"You were leading a combat patrol," Ernie said. "Things like that happen during a combat patrol. What was your alternative? To just sit down out there in the jungle for two days, then come back?"

"I could've had better recon," Hunter said.

"I hear you called for an air recon just before you were hit."

"Yeah, but he didn't see anything. Hell, it was just a chopper, probably on some routine supply run somewhere. I shouldn't have depended on that."

"Nevertheless, he was in a position to see, and he didn't see anything. You made your decision on the best available information. Besides, you didn't really come out that bad." Ernie smiled. "I'll bet Custer would trade places with you."

"I got your Custer." Hunter laughed, grabbing his scrotum. "Hanging."

Francis W. Poindexter opened his eyes and tried to figure out where he was. He was in a bed somewhere, but it wasn't his tent at An Loi. There was a ceiling overhead, a real ceiling, with bright lights. The room was cool, almost cold, so he knew it was air-conditioned. A woman was standing over his bed, looking down at him. She was wearing fatigues and there was a first lieutenant's bar on her collar.

He knew where he was then. He remembered. He looked toward his left arm and saw that it was elevated with slings and pulleys. He could feel his arm being stretched.

"My arm!" he said. "You saved my arm? But how? I saw it . . ."

"I'm sorry, Francis," the nurse said, using his first name. "It's gone."

Francis looked at the rigging on the left side of his body. "I can feel it," he said. "I can see it."

"What you feel is called 'ghost sensation.' You just think you feel your arm. And what you are seeing is a traction arrangement designed to pull your skin over the stump so it will heal cleanly."

Francis turned his head away from the rigging and traction. He lay quiet for a few moments.

"I'm sorry," the nurse said. "Can I get you anything?"

"Yeah," Francis said. "A new arm."

"I'll be back if you need me," the nurse said. She turned and walked away from the bed and Francis saw a sheen of tears in her eyes. He had made her cry. Well, fuck her. She wasn't the one laid up without an arm, he was.

An orderly brought a couple of pills by a few moments later, and shortly after Francis took the pills he went back to sleep, to dream:

"Francis? Francis, it's time to get up. You don't want to be late for school." Francis's mother came up the stairs and pushed open the door to his room. She turned on the lights.

"I'm awake, Mom, I'm awake," Francis mumbled. He looked around at his room, at the pennants and pictures on the wall. On his trophy case were the dozens of trophies he had won swimming. On the back of the mirror was a pair of red-and-black panties. He had convinced his mother they were a joke, though in fact Marriane had been wearing them the night he finally broke down her defenses.

Francis stumbled out of bed. He was wearing fatigues, jungle boots, web belt, complete with canteen, first-aid pack, ammo pouches, and knife. He had on a flak jacket and half a dozen grenades and was carrying an M-16. He went down to the kitchen, where his mother was making pancakes.

"Oh, Francis," she said. "Where's your arm? You're bleeding all over the floor. What happened to your arm? Didn't I tell you to be careful?"

Francis awakened with a start.

"Hey, my man, you okay?" It was a black soldier in the bed next to him.

"Yeah," Francis said. He closed his eyes for a moment. "I was having a dream."

"A strange dream, right? Where things get all mixed up and you don't know what's real and what's not?" the black soldier asked.

"Yeah."

"It's those fuckin' pills, man. You don't want to take too many of them. They'll fuck your mind up bad."

The black man's name was Shuler. He had driven his Jeep over a homemade mine, and his thighs, stomach, and groin had caught a load of shrapnel.

Shuler filled Francis in on the hospital staff. Lieutenant Swift, the nurse on duty now and the one Francis had met earlier, was an "all right" officer. There was a captain who was a pain in the ass, though Shuler admitted that she may have just been around too long. "They see all the blood and dyin' and all and it fucks up their minds. You know what I mean?"

The meals were being served by hospital orderlies, and when one of the orderlies set Francis's supper in front of him, he turned up his nose.

"What is this shit?" he asked. "When can I have some real food?"

"I don't know," the orderly said. "I just know what's on your chart now."

"I'll take care of this, Vanders," Lieutenant Swift said. She walked up to Francis and smiled at him. "You can have real food tomorrow, if you want it."

"Yeah, sure I want to."

"Good. That's a good sign," she said. She opened

the little container of broth, then positioned the tray so he could reach it and the spoon. "Would you like some ice cream a little later on?"

"Yeah," Francis said. He smiled. "It's been weeks since we had any ice cream up at An Loi." He laughed. "I finally make it to Saigon and I'm laid up in the damned hospital. What about the other guys who got hit with me this morning? Are they here, too?"

"Yes. Only you weren't hit this morning. You were hit Tuesday morning. This is Friday evening."

"This is Friday? You mean it's been four days since I was hit?"

"Yes."

"My, my. Time certainly flies when you're having a good time," Francis said.

The nurse laughed, and Francis remembered then that he had made her cry earlier in the day.

"Listen," he said. "If I mouthed off, or said anything I shouldn't have, I'm sorry," he said. "I didn't mean anything by it."

"Don't worry," she said. "I have thick skin."

Francis lifted his hand and rubbed his fingers across her cheek. "You have pretty skin, I'll give you that," he said.

"There you go," she teased. "You come to Saigon, you figure you just have to make out, so if you can't go downtown you'll hit on anybody."

Francis chuckled. "That's the way of it," he said. "By the way, how are the other guys who came in with me?"

"Meagher and Billings are fine. They keep asking about you. They're over in Ward Two. They'll come see you tomorrow if you're up to it."

"Hell, I'm up to it, I'm up to it. Tell them to come on," Francis said. "What about Mike?"

The nurse moved the empty broth cup and slid the Jell-O over in front of him. She was silent, and Francis knew what that meant. He stared at the little green squares as they laid there like jiggling emeralds.

"I'm sorry, Francis," the nurse said. "Specialist Spears died this morning."

Francis was quiet for a long moment. "I was feeling sorry for myself because I lost my arm," he said. "I guess Mike would trade with me if he could."

"I thought we had an understanding," Lieutenant Cox said. He had Staff Sergeant Mills in his hooch. "I thought you were going to call me in if you got into any trouble."

"Yes, sir," Mills said. He was puzzled by the way the conversation was going. "But we didn't get into any trouble."

"You got four men blown away," Cox said. "What the hell do you call that?"

"Sir, they were casualties, just like any other casualties," Mills said. "Sergeant Two Bears called in Dustoff, just like he was supposed to. And he made sure the area was secure before he called them in. I couldn't see that he was doing anything wrong."

"Then you obviously don't have the kind of foresight I'm looking for in a leader," Lieutenant Cox said.

"Sir, I don't understand."

"It's obvious to me that you don't understand,"

Cox said. "Never mind. It wasn't a major disaster. I guess, all things considered, all's well that ends well. Now, you're sure the troops you encountered weren't NVA?"

"Yes, sir, I'm sure."

"Doesn't it seem odd to run into so many V.C.?"

"Yes, sir. But Hunter says this is the hardcore element of all the V.C. in this sector. He says they're raising more hell than the Ghost Patrol, and they're the ones we should be going after. He's upset because the colonel won't see it that way. The colonel's still set on us going after the Ghost Patrol."

"The colonel's right," Cox said. "The Ghost Patrol is exactly what you should be going after."

# Chapter Nine

Captain Minh and Sergeant Phat of the People's Army of Vietnam (V.C.) rode the An Loi–Saigon bus into Saigon. The bus was packed with as many as one hundred people, including the ones who dangled out the windows and rode standing on the back bumper, hanging onto whatever they could grab hold of.

The top of the bus was laden heavily with personal belongings: boxes, baskets, a bicycle, a sewing machine, a cluster of chickens tide together by their legs, a couple of goats lying down calmly, unsurprised by anything that happened to them.

While the bus was going, an old woman who had been sitting in a seat in front of Minh made a laborious exit through one of the windows and pulled herself painfully up the side of the bus and over the top. At one point she slipped and slid all the way to the bottom, where she managed to grab hold at the last second and hang there with the pavement just inches away, flashing beneath her at forty miles an hour.

No one offered to help, and after hanging there for a short while, the old woman improved her position enough to begin her climb anew. When she finally reached the top, she fell out across the baggage, breathing heavily. She caught her breath, straightened her black pajamas, and began rummaging through the baskets until she found the one she was after. She reached down inside, pulled out a raw turnip, then, slowly and carefully, crawled back down the side of the bus and reentered the window. Though her seat had been filled in her absence, she squeezed her way back into it, then sat there, calmly munching on the turnip for her lunch.

Minh and Phat proceeded directly to Cholon, where they boarded the *Peaceful Journey*, not a ship, but a large, oceangoing ark. The boat was unpainted except for the name and the great evil eye that was put there to ward off any wicked spirits that might come to plague it. A gangplank stretched from the boat to the wooded dock, and men and women alike moved up and down the wet boards, bent over under the load of their sacks of rice.

Half a dozen soldiers stood by in varying degrees of attentiveness, watching the proceedings. Ostensibly they were there to check for possible deserters or smugglers, but a five-hundred-plaster note would turn their heads long enough for any illegal transaction to take place.

Minh slipped an orange five-hundred-P note to

the soldier nearest the gangplank, who turned to watch a small skiff on the river as Minh and Phat went inside the boat.

The interior of the boat was dank and unpleasant. It had one large planked deck of damp, smelly wood and it was packed with people. Whole families had spread blankets on that portion of the deck to which they laid claim as their own. They surrounded themselves with possessions, not only those things they were taking to their destination, but the provisions necessary to sustain them during the week-long voyage. The air was rancid with the smell of dried fish, molding cheese, excrement from frightened dogs and chickens, and rotting vegetables.

Minh and Phat found a place for themselves, then settled down to wait for the voyage to begin. Like the others, they had brought their own food: cooked rice and bits of fish wrapped securely in palm-tree fronds.

Several hours later the boat was rocking its way through the South China Sea. Minh stood up and walked to one of the portholes, picking his way gingerly through the clusters of people who were squatting on the deck, laughing and talking. He looked through the glassless opening and saw the coast, a verdant green shoreline some five miles distant. He watched it for a while, then returned to sit beside Phat. Phat moved over slightly to make room for him.

Minh and Phat had taken the trip to Saigon, then boarded this boat, because it was going to be hijacked just off the coast of Phan Thiet the next morning. Ten skiffs, carrying five men each, would intercept the boat just before dawn. They would force the captain to put in to shore, where the people would be taken off the boat, and the boat would be loaded with weapons and ammunition to take up the Mekong to be distributed to V.C. battalions in the area.

If everything went as planned, it would be a smooth operation. If fighting broke out, the fifty well-armed men would be able to handle it, especially with Minh and Phat working from the inside.

"The passengers will be disturbed, but, if they make no trouble, they won't be hurt," Minh had explained to Phat when he transmitted the orders to him. "Anyway, it's for them that we do this thing. Don't forget, we are fighting for their freedom."

That had been yesterday, when they were planning the operation. Now, as he looked around at the passengers, he wondered about it.

"Phat," he said. "Look around you."

"What?" Phat asked. "What do you wish me to see?"

"These people," Minh said. "Is it worth the suffering we are going through for these people? Look at them. They are like sheep."

"You said we are fighting for them."

"I know, I know. But sometimes I wonder if it is all worth it. Look at them. I don't think half of them even know what country they are in. Or care. And the information they get comes from the lies the government tells them."

"Someday they will know the truth," Phat said.

"What is the truth?" Minh asked. He sighed. "For them truth is the truth of momentary reality.

They make a hole in the field, plant rice, spread that field with shit, and flood it with water. That's all they really care about. We fight and die for them, yet we are treated as the enemy, as something unclean. It gives one pause for thought, don't you think?''

"Has your resolve weakened?" Phat asked.

"No," Minh answered. "My resolve is as strong as it has ever been. It is their resolve I'm worried about. Suppose we win freedom for them. Are they ready for it?''

"I don't know," Phat said.

"I can tell you. They are not. There must be many years of strong leadership and education before the people can be trusted with their own destiny.''

"Who will provide that leadership?" Phat asked.

"Why, we shall, of course," Minh answered. "That is, those of us who survive the battle. Those who die must be an inspiration for the others.''

Phat smiled. "I think I would rather be a leader than an inspiration," he said.

Minh and Phat grew quiet after that, each of them lost in his own thoughts. The sun that had been streaming in through the portholes and cracks during the afternoon faded away into that peculiar Vietnamese evening that knew no twilight but merely went from light to dark. Throughout the boat, lanterns were lit and conversations grew subdued as shadows gathered around the golden glows of kerosene lamps. The passengers were eating their evening meal.

Minh took two of the palm-wrapped rice packages and handed one to Phat.

"It's good," Phat said. He smiled. "We have eaten much worse in the field."

"Yes, but once we ate grandly. Do you remember?" Minh asked. "We attacked the 15th Special Infantry and the commander had just set an elegant feast."

Phat chuckled. "Ah, yes, I remember that well. Never have I eaten as well as we ate that day."

"And yet, you will remember, such food was only for the officers," Minh reminded him. "The soldiers had rice, such as we are having now."

"Not as good, I would say," Phat said, using his fingers to shove the last bit of rice into his mouth. He licked his lips appreciatively.

After their meal, they lay down in their space, and a short while later Minh was lulled to sleep by the gentle rocking of the boat and the quiet throb of the engine. Sometime around three in the morning, he was awakened by the frightened voice of a woman and the gentle murmurings of Phat.

Minh sat up and saw that the woman was holding a baby. The baby was naked and dirty and its puffy little eyes were swollen shut. The baby's skin looked to be red.

"What is it?" Minh asked. "What is wrong?"

"The baby is sick," Phat said. "The woman has asked me if I know anyone who can help."

Minh reached out and touched the baby's skin. It was burning.

"He has a fever," Minh said. "Perhaps if we take him on deck and bathe him with cool seawater we can bring down the temperature. Do you wish us to try?" he asked the woman.

"Yes," the woman said.

The stars were spread brightly across the sky and the moon hung like a great silver orb, splashing a shining pathway that stretched from the horizon to the shore. The breeze was refreshingly cool after the stuffy hold, and Minh was glad they had come on deck.

Phat got a bucket of cool seawater and Minh began bathing the baby with it. The baby screamed at first, then began whimpering again. After half an hour the whimpers turned to sighs, and Minh stood up, holding the baby in his arms. The baby opened its eyes and looked into Minh's face, and Minh could see that the eyes were clear and healthy-looking in the lantern light.

"Thank you," the woman babbled over and over again as she took the baby back. "Thank you."

"We have won the gratitude of that woman," Phat said. "But I fear we will lose it when our people attack the boat at dawn."

"If it is to be, it is to be," Minh said.

Minh awakened Phat awhile later. When Phat opened his eyes, Minh put his fingers to his lips to signal quiet.

"It is nearly dawn," Minh said. "We should go on deck now."

Phat followed Minh up the ladder and back out onto the deck. In the east, a thin bar of red broke over the South China Sea. To the west the land was little more than a dark shadow. Then, gradually, like shadows moving within shadows, Minh and Phat saw the approaching boats. They were long and slim, and they moved quickly across the water, propelled not by their outboard motors, which would have given them away, but rowed by the men on the boats.

"There they are," Minh said. "Now, we must stop this boat."

Minh and Phat walked back to the stern of the boat. There the pilot stood by the tiller, while an old woman, probably his wife, worked at a charcoal stove cooking his breakfast soup. The pilot saw Minh and Phat approaching.

"You are up early," the pilot said.

"Yes," Minh answered. He pulled a pistol and pointed it at the pilot. "I'm afraid it has to do with our job. If you would be so kind as to stop the boat, please?"

"Are you pirates?"

"We are fighters for the National Liberation Front."

The pilot breathed a sigh of relief. Then he smiled. "In that case I am your friend," he said. "I feared you were pirates. What would you have me do?"

"We are going to use your boat for a while," Minh said. "We have some weapons we wish to transport."

"The passengers," the pilot said. "When they see the weapons, they will talk."

"The passengers will be put ashore before the weapons are loaded," Minh explained. "Stop the engine, please. Our friends will be aboard momentarily."

The approaching boats touched alongside a few moments later, and forty men boarded, leaving only one man per boat. The boarders moved quickly to establish control of the big boat, and less than ten minutes after they boarded, all passengers were disarmed and the pilot was heading for shore.

"Phat," Minh called a few moments later. Phat had been moving among the passengers, assuring them that those who cooperated would not be hurt. Phat had been talking with the assault team leader.

"Yes?"

"Take the passengers ashore, far enough away from the boat that they can't see anything. We don't want any information getting back to the authorities."

"Very well," Phat agreed.

When they reached shore the gangplank was lowered and all the passengers — the old men and old women, the children, and the babies — were moved off the boat. They shuffled down the gangplank carrying their belongings with them, moving stoically, as if this were no more than a routine stop in their journey. Phat walked with them, leading them about five kilometers away from the shore. He told them to set down there and wait for his return. Then he left. Of course, he had no intention of returning, but by the time they realized that, the business at the boat would be done.

When Phat returned to the boat he saw men loading weapons. He looked back toward the tiller and saw a new pilot.

"Where is the other pilot?" he asked.

Minh pointed down, and Phat saw two bodies floating face down in the backwater. One was the pilot; the other was his wife.

"You killed them?"

"Yes," Minh said.

"But they were cooperating with us."

"Perhaps. He may also have been merely pretending to cooperate with us so he could provide the government with information," Minh said. "We had no choice, we had to stick with the plan."

Phat looked down at the bodies. The woman was still clutching her cooking spoon.

"Med Evac 717, you are cleared for immediate departure runway two-seven. Turn right as soon as possible after takeoff, contact Paris Control."

"Roger, Ton Son Nhut, Med Evac 717 rolling."

Four turboprop engines were advanced to full military takeoff power as the C-130 started down the runway. The propeller blade tips cut swirls through the mist so that long corkscrew contrails followed the airplane down the runway until it rotated, then climbed out of Ton Son Nhut at a 45-degree angle.

There were eighty-seven people on board the C-130 as it winged its way to Tokyo. Up front there were two pilots, a flight engineer, and a radio-navigator. In addition there were two airmen crew chiefs. There were also four doctors and eight nurses on board. The rest of the passengers were patients. All the patients were stretcher cases, and the stretchers were triple-decked along both sides of the airplane. Francis Poindexter was in one of the stretchers.

"How are we feeling?" one of the doctors asked, stopping by Francis's stretcher and putting his hand on his forehead.

"We are feeling fine," Francis said quietly and without expression.

"Good, good," the doctor said. "That is good." The doctor moved to the next stretcher and asked the same question, to receive the same noncommittal answer, and he responded in the same way. "Good, good, that is good."

Francis listened to the doctor's "good, good" float up the aisle until the worthy doctor moved far enough away so that the constant drone of the engines drowned him out. Francis turned and looked through the window. He could see the lower surface of the high wing, the bulge of the two engine nacelles, and the externally carried fuel tank, which hung on the wing between the two engines. He looked at the ailerons, saw a tiny movement, and thought of the pilot sitting up front, all comfortable and content, driving this thing with no more effort than driving a car. He saw the nylon static electricity leads stretching out from the trailing edge of the wing and he wondered why the three-hundred-fifty-mile-an-hour wind didn't tear them off. By turning his head slightly, he could look down. He could see nothing but clouds, though once, when the clouds parted slightly, he saw a mantle of green and he wondered if they were still over Vietnam. If so, was some infantryman slogging around down there, sucking his feet out of the mire and muck of flooded rice fields, slapping at mosquitoes, twitching every time he passed a hooch or a clump of trees, or anywhere else a V.C. might hide?

At least he wasn't down there now. He paid a hell of a price to get out, but at least he wasn't down there.

"How are we feeling?" one of the doctors asked.

Francis looked over at him. This wasn't the same doctor.

"We are feeling fine," Francis said quietly and without expression.

"Good, good," the doctor said. "That is good." The doctor moved to the next stretcher and asked the same question. Francis couldn't hear the patient's answer, but he heard the doctor.

"Good, good. That is good."

# Chapter Ten

At 1800 hours an ambush patrol left An Loi, just as it did every night. This night the ambush patrol was the same size as Sergeant Two Bears's Rape and Pillage platoon. It was hoped that the Vietnamese who were in the camp by day, and were V.C. by night, would think it was the same platoon.

In fact, at 2200 hours, long after all the Vietnamese were gone from the compound, Hunter's platoon left by an auxiliary gate. They moved quickly and silently away from the village, through the thin jungle and across dozens of open rice paddies, staying on the dikes so they wouldn't be slowed down by the flooded fields. For the first several kilometers they avoided all contact, swinging wide of farm hooches, ducking for cover when they saw a light.

Hunter kept them moving at a steady pace for four hours, resting them from 0200 to 0300. At 0300 they moved out again and kept up a steady march until just before dawn, at which time they crossed over into Cambodia. Hunter considered the consequences of being in Cambodia. One moment ago they were soldiers, out on patrol. Now they were criminals, violating neutral territory. At best, they were now subject to court-martial and imprisonment. At worst, they could broaden the war.

They continued on, going deeper and deeper into Cambodia. The jungle was thick here and the going was difficult and tangled with undergrowth. Sometimes it was so thick that they literally had to hack their way through the brush. It was hot and their energy was sapped, not only by the muggy heat, but by the mosquitoes that swarmed around them. The men gulped their water and Hunter had to caution them about water conservation.

Pepper was on point, and about ten kilometers after they crossed the Cambodian border, he halted. Hunter crawled forward, passing the others, who had dropped into hiding places as soon as the patrol stopped moving.

Hunter found Pepper on his belly, under a tree, looking over a small rise.

"What is it?" he asked.

Pepper pointed ahead. "This is what we came for," he said.

In a small clearing ahead, Hunter saw what Pepper was talking about. It was a base camp, not unlike An Loi, though this was considerably smaller.

The camp was surrounded by concertina wire and there were guard towers at all four corners. There were three long buildings that might have been barracks, a small building that housed the camp generator, and two smaller buildings, probably the headquarters building and the officers' quarters. There were no flags, nor were there any vehicles or other equipment with insignia of any sort, but Hunter knew that the men in this camp were North Vietnamese soldiers.

"Sergeant Mills to the front," he called. His call was passed quietly to Mills, and a moment later Mills came up beside him.

"Tell the mortars to take out the barracks and generator house. Put the rocket launchers on the guard towers."

"Right," Mills answered.

"I'll get everyone else deployed with the best possible field of fire. Then we'll take targets of opportunity."

"When do we start?"

"Right after sunup," Hunter said. "I'll break squelch three times."

"Okay."

"Mills?"

"Yes?"

Hunter stroked his chin and looked at the younger NCO. "You know we're in Cambodia, don't you?" he asked.

"I figured we might be," Mills said.

"I just wanted you to know," Hunter said. "If anything happens to me, you're in charge. You're going to have to get the men back across the border as fast as you can."

"Right," Mills answered. "Sergeant Two Bears?"

"Yes."

"Try and stay around, okay? I don't want to be in charge."

"What's the matter? No ambition?" Hunter teased.

"There you go," Mills replied. He crawled back to get the heavy-weapons people in position. Hunter began spreading out the rest of the men. When everyone was ready, they waited.

Hunter found a can of fruit cocktail and opened it slowly with his P-38. He drank the juice first, enjoying the cool sweetness. After the juice was drunk, he ate the little pieces of fruit, delighting in the texture and the moistness as much as the taste. He didn't know why the army didn't put the canned fruit in every C-ration unit. It was far and away the best thing in the entire inventory, and never had it been more delicious than it was right now.

He wondered why he was enjoying it so much. He could be at the Top of The Mark in San Francisco, or Antoine's in New Orleans, and not enjoy a meal more than he was enjoying this one. The beef stew and Indian fry bread his mother used to cook for him wasn't as good as this little tin of fruit cocktail. It was true, what they said: Life did have more sweetness when death was near.

Just after sunup, someone came out of one of the barracks and walked over to the row of concentina wire to take a leak. He was joined by another, then another, until soon fifteen or twenty men were standing there, some finishing and starting back to the barracks, but others taking their place immediately. A radio was playing in the barracks and the whining, nasal sound of Vietnamese music could be heard. The camp was totally unaware they were in any danger. Even the men in the guard towers were lax. One of them came down from the tower to get his breakfast, while the others were looking back into the camp toward the morning routine, rather than away from the camp as they should be.

Hunter smiled. It was obvious that they were counting on the Cambodian border to provide them with all the protection they needed. It was a pretty sweet setup they had. They could leave here, hit a target in Vietnam less than an hour later, then beat a hasty retreat back across the border to the safety of Cambodia.

A least that's what they assumed. Hunter was about to demonstrate to the North Vietnamese that the old military axiom "Assumption is the mother of fuck-ups" was true.

Hunter broke squelch on the radio once, twice, three times. At the third time he heard the hollow *kerchung* of mortars being fired. Seconds later there were four explosions inside the camp, two of them direct hits on the barracks. He saw the plumes of rocket smoke as the 3.5 rocket launchers were fired at the guard towers. All four towers disappeared in a rose of flame and a plume of smoke.

"Fire!" Hunter shouted. "Open fire!"

The M-16's and the M-60 machine guns started popping away, and tracer rounds slashed down into the camp.

The North Vietnamese were caught completely by surprise and they started running pell-mell around the compound. It was almost thirty seconds before any return fire came back from the camp, and when it did it was pitifully weak.

Hunter kept it up, pouring in the small-arms fire. The mortars found their range and, one after another, the buildings in the compound were destroyed. In addition, the M-79's found their range and were dropping right in the middle of the NVA troops. Finally, Hunter saw a handful of North Vietnamese soldiers fleeing from the other side of the camp. He ordered them fired on and the tracer rounds from his men chased the North Vietnamese into the jungle on the opposite side of the camp.

"Cease fire! Cease fire!" Hunter called.

It took a second, but all firing stopped. For a moment there was absolute silence, for the gunfire had quieted even the jungle creatures. Hunter swept the camp with his binoculars. He saw no sign of life. He raised the PRC-6 to his lips.

"Mills?"

"Yeah, I'm here."

"Any casualties?"

"None."

"All right. I'm taking half the platoon in. You stay back to cover us. If you hear anyone coming, give us a call."

"Roger," Mills answered.

"Come on," Hunter said to those around him. "Let's go down and see what we can find."

Hunter and Pepper broke the advancing squad into groups of three men each. Cautiously, they worked their way down toward the camp, keeping to the cover of trees and bushes, darting from one to the other as quickly as they could. When they reached the perimeter of the camp, Hunter signaled the others down, while he advanced alone.

Crawling right up to the concertina, Hunter looked for mines, either pressure or command-detonated. He found neither, more evidence of the fact that the NVA figured they were safe inside the Cambodian border. He found a break in the concertina wire, then went through it. When he was on the other side, he signaled for the others to come on through.

As the other men came into the compound, Hunter started moving carefully through it. There were dozens of bodies scattered around, most in the underwear in which they had slept. Hunter moved through them, searching carefully for any indications of mines or booby traps. He saw the generator shack, destroyed by his mortar crews. The generator was in pieces.

The headquarters building, like the other buildings, had sustained heavy damage from the mortar shells. However, it was made of cinder blocks, and so was still, substantially, intact. Hunter signaled for Pepper to cover him as he approached the building. He stopped just outside the door and tossed in a hand grenade. After the grenade went off, he dashed inside.

This building, like the others, was deserted. He did notice something of interest, however. There was a bulletin board on one wall, plastered with newspaper articles. The articles were from American newspapers, and they were all about the Ghost Patrol.

"Pepper," Hunter called, "get in here."

Pepper came through the door, stepping over the debris and one NVA body.

"Take a look," Hunter said, pointing to the bulletin board.

"I'll be a son of a bitch," Pepper said. "These fuckers were keeping a scrapbook."

"You got that little camera with you?"

"Yeah."

"Get a picture," Hunter said. "I want to show that shit to the colonel when we get back."

Pepper took out his camera and began snapping pictures. Hunter started pulling open file cabinet drawers looking for maps, or anything he might find that could be of value. The only worthwhile thing he found was a bottle of whiskey.

Back in An Loi, Spec-Four McKay looked up as Sergeant Bill Hanlon stepped into the orderly room.

"What the hell are you doing here?" McKay asked in surprise. "I thought you got out."

"I did," Bill said. "I came back."

"You're crazy, you know that? I mean, you were out of here . . . really out of here. Back in the world as a civilian. Now you're here."

"Yeah, now I'm here," Bill said. "So, enough about that, already. Where's Sergeant Two Bears?"

"He's in the field."

"No sweat. Just put me down for his platoon and I'll wait for him to come back."

"I'm afraid there's no room in his platoon,"

McKay said, looking at the manning chart. "His platoon's been augmented, it's full."

"What do you mean there's no room? I'm the squad leader, second squad."

"Not anymore," McKay said. "That's Sergeant Conroy's squad now."

"So, hell, move Conroy somewhere else."

Lieutenant Cox overheard Hanlon and McKay, and he stepped out of his office.

"So you're back, I see," he said.

"Lieutenant Cox," Hanlon said. "You're my platoon leader. Tell McKay where I belong."

"I'm not the platoon leader anymore," Cox said. "I'm the CO."

That news startled Bill, but he didn't show it. He smiled. "Well, then, that's even better. You know where I belong."

"Put him in the third platoon," Cox said.

"Third platoon?"

"You'll do a good job there, Hanlon," Lieutenant Cox said. "And I need some experience there. I'm getting the platoon ready for a special mission."

"Yes, sir," Bill said. He knew better than to carry his protest any further. Anyway, he was back in Vietnam, back where he wanted to be. He'd just let it go at that. "When will Hunter be back?"

"I can't tell you, exactly," Lieutenant Cox said. "He's on an extended patrol."

"An extended patrol?"

"He went after the Ghost Patrol," McKay said.

"Shit!" Bill said. "And I'm not with him."

"Don't worry, Sergeant Hanlon, I promise you enough action to keep you interested," Cox said mysteriously.

For Hunter and the Rape and Pillage platoon, the trip back was proving to be uneventful. They didn't use the same route leaving Cambodia they had used coming in, because Hunter feared that the surviving NVA might have found it and set up an ambush. That was what he would have done, and he credited the NVA commander with at least as much sense as he had.

By a fluke, the way back was much easier. They struck out through rice fields, little patches of jungle, and streams as easily as going on a field march back in the States. Hunter moved fast, but with flankers out to look for the enemy. None were found and they crossed back into Vietnam without contact.

By 1630 hours, Hunter and the Rape and Pillage platoon were coming through the main gate. He had left with thirty-eight men; he was coming back with thirty-eight men. No one killed, no one wounded. As soon as he came through the gate he was told to report to Colonel Petery.

"I don't encourage this sort of thing during duty hours," Colonel Petery said, as he opened his file cabinet. "But the sun is over the yardarm, as our naval friends say, so, Sergeant, how about a drink?"

"Thank you, sir, don't mind if I do," Hunter said.

"You, Lieutenant Cox?"

"Yes, sir, thank you," Cox answered.

Colonel Petery poured both men a drink, then poured one for himself. He corked the bottle and returned it to the file cabinet. Hunter couldn't help but smile. That was the same place the NVA commander was hiding his whiskey. Maybe all commanders were alike.

"Tell me about the mission," Colonel Petery said.

"We located the NVA base camp," Hunter said.

"Where?"

"About ten clicks on the other side of the Cambodian border."

"No, you didn't," Colonel Petery said.

"Beg your pardon, sir?"

"You weren't on the other side of the border," Colonel Petery said.

"I wasn't?"

Colonel Petery took a drink of his whiskey and looked over the rim at Hunter. "You aren't sure where the base camp is. After all, you were a little disoriented. All you are certain of is that it was on the Vietnamese side of the border."

"Very well, sir," Hunter said.

"Look, Sergeant, I don't think the North Vietnamese are going to say anything about this. According to their propaganda, there are no North Vietnamese in the war at all. It is all a popular uprising of the people, or some such shit as that. You think they're going to raise hell because one of their base camps was destroyed?"

"I don't know," Hunter said.

"Believe me, they won't say a word. The ones we have to worry about are the antiwar people in our own country. Go on with your report."

"Nothing else to report," Hunter said. "We hit them early this morning. The camp was pretty much destroyed. There were several NVA killed. We had no casualties."

"Hot damn!" Colonel Petery said, hitting his fist in his palm. "I knew you could do the job. I knew it!"

"Congratulations, Sergeant," Lieutenant Cox said, sticking out his hand. "I want you to know that I am putting you in for the Silver Star."

"I didn't do anything to earn the Silver Star," Hunter said.

"You let us be the judge of that," Cox said. "Colonel Petery has already approved the recommendation, and it's gone forward. I just hope my own mission is as successful."

"Your mission, sir?"

"Yes," Colonel Petery said. "I've approved another mission like the one you just completed, only this one is to go after the core element of V.C. in the area."

"As soon as your men get a little rest," Lieutenant Cox said, "we're going out in company strength."

"Very well, sir," Hunter said.

"By the way, we just got a new replacement in," Cox said, smiling. "I'm sure you'll be interested in him."

"Who is it?"

"Sergeant Bill Hanlon."

"What? I thought he got out," Hunter said.

"The way I understand it, he was out for all of two weeks. He's back, bright-eyed, bushy-tailed, and ready to go."

"In my platoon?"

"Uh . . . no, I put him in the third platoon," Cox said. "I need the experience there."

"I'll trade you one of my experienced men for him."

"He's mine, no matter where he is, Sergeant Two Bears," Cox said crisply. "Don't forget, it's my company. And I prefer to keep him in the third platoon."

"Yes, sir," Hunter said.

Cox drained the rest of his drink. "I'd better see to the ambush patrol. Sergeant, we'll talk tomorrow. I'm sure you'll have some valuable information to share."

"Yes, sir."

Colonel Petery waited until Cox was gone before he spoke again. Finally, he sighed.

"I had to give him this operation," Colonel Petery said. "He was ready to submit a request through channels to the next higher. I couldn't afford to have them looking too closely at what we're doing here. They might have found out about your little jaunt into Cambodia."

"Couldn't you find anyone else to command it?" Hunter asked. "That man is an asshole."

"But he is an officer in the United States Army," Colonel Petery said. "And I would appreciate it if you would remember that."

"Yes, sir. That's not something I'm likely to forget, Colonel," Hunter said grimly.

# Chapter Eleven

The C-130 landed at Tachikawa Air Force Base near Yokohama, Japan. The rear door went down and the stretcher cases and walking wounded were transferred to hospital buses that came from the 106th General Army Hospital.

Though there was nothing wrong with Francis Poindexter's legs, the wound over the end of his arm was still open and draining, necessitating that it be immobilized. Therefore, he was confined to a stretcher.

Francis had missed Japan on the way over, and had never seen the country. He chuckled, dryly. This was a hell of a way to visit. He raised himself up a little to look out the window. The streets were alive with people, busy people hurrying to and fro on whatever personal errands took them about.

The thing he noticed most was the way they felt no sense of danger. But it was tiring to hold his head up, so, with a sigh, he let it fall back to the stretcher and stared at the tiny holes on the ceiling of the bus.

Once in the hospital, the doctors were able to close his arm stump. When he awoke in his bed the next morning, he was aware, perhaps for the first time, that he would be minus one arm for the rest of his life. He knew it was an irrational thought, but as long as the wound was open, he had not fully accepted the loss.

Within a few days, Francis began adjusting to the situation. Through his window he could hear the sounds of peaceful street traffic. The halls were filled with smiling doctors and nurses, the sheets were clean, and the food was good. As a young, pretty nurse cut his pork chops for him, he thought of the guys back in An Loi and wondered what they were eating. It was odd. He was here physically, but mentally he was still in the jungle with his unit. He couldn't get over the feeling that he was expected back, that his bunk was still there in the tent and his buddies were waiting for him. He owed Mitchell five dollars. Silverthorn owed him three.

Two weeks later, Francis was loaded onto a hospital bus with a dozen other patients. This time Francis was walking, and he sat in a seat near the window so he could look out. A triple amputee, no more than nineteen, was loaded onto a stretcher beside him. A hospital corpsman was with him, holding a can of root beer. The young amputee was sucking the root beer through a straw. Seeing him, Francis felt almost guilty that he was coming out of country in so much better shape.

At the air base they were loaded onto a C-141. The C-141 was the largest airplane Francis had ever seen, and it was like being moved into a gymnasium. Francis was taken to a seat and told to sit down. Because of his arm, he was given an isolated seat so there would be little danger of anyone bumping into him. He sat quietly, listening to sounds of the airplane being loaded: the snapping of locks as the stretchers were secured, the closing of seat belts, and finally the whine of the big rear door as it was closed. A few moments later the jet engines roared as the ship rumbled down the runway and finally lifted off. There were no cheers.

Captain Minh lay on the sleeping mat beside the young girl who had proudly given her body to a hero of the revolution last night. After delivering the weapons, he was asked to go to Tuy Duc, where he met with Major Dom, of the NVA. Major Dom was upset because the Americans had attacked an NVA camp across the border in Cambodia and he wanted Captain Minh to conduct an operation to "punish" the Americans for their sins.

Captain Minh looked over at the young girl. He had no idea how old she was, though she didn't look much more than seventeen. Her breasts were little more than slight pillows of flesh, though her nipples were the nipples of a woman. She had been proud of her ability to please him last night, and now she slept the peaceful sleep of one who had done her best to serve the cause. She had called him a "hero" last night.

*You think what I do is heroic?* Minh thought as he looked at the sleeping girl. He reached down and brushed her long hair away from her face so he could see her. *The battle against mosquitoes and snakes and all sorts of biting insects is not heroic. The battle against skin diseases and malaria and dysentery is not heroic. It is not heroic to be hungry and wet, and to suffer from the heat, and yet, all these things we must do. It is not even heroic to fight against the Americans when you lose the element of surprise and the American firepower and numbers can become very deadly. I am not a hero, I am an accident.*

The girl moved against Minh, and feeling the pressure of her body against his made him aware that his bladder was full. He got up from the mat and walked to the door to relieve himself. That was when he saw them. So high that they were practically invisible, a flight of B-52's was coming toward them. There were nine planes in three groups of three. The first three banked away sharply, and he wondered why. Then he realized that this village was very close to the Cambodian border, and the airplanes would have to turn sharply to keep from overflying the border. That hadn't stopped the soldiers who attacked the NVA camp, but they had slipped in, then slipped out. Bombers couldn't do that.

Minh wondered why they were here. The second V of three aircraft banked away, then the third V.

Suddenly Minh got a sinking sensation in the pit of his stomach. Those planes were dropping bombs! He couldn't see anything yet, but he knew it. Within a couple of minutes the bombs would come crashing down on the village!

"Awake!" he shouted. "Everyone awake! Find shelter! B-52's! We are being bombed by B-52's!"

The young girl with whom he had spent the night was up instantly. Her eyes were wide with fear.

"Bombs!" Minh shouted. "We've got to find shelter!"

"Come!" the girl said, and she darted out the back of the hut, with Minh right behind her. The girl ran toward a tree, then dropped down and disappeared beneath a bush. Minh realized there must be a hole there, and he went with her.

Minh's shouts had awakened a few others, and they in turn shouted at others, so that the village was awake and everyone was running toward some sort of shelter.

By now Minh's fears were realized, because the bombs had fallen far enough so that the whistle of their fall could be heard. It would be less than thirty seconds now before the first bombs hit.

The girl beside Minh drew next to him in terror. If she looked seventeen last night, she looked no more than twelve at this moment, and Minh reached for her, not as he would toward a woman with whom he had just spent the night, but as he would for a child.

"We will be all right in here," he said reassuringly, though he knew that their chances were not very good, even in this shelter.

The first bombs hit. They fell in the jungle at least half a mile from the village, and the thunder of their explosions was deafening. Smoke and flame rose above the point of the bomb strikes, and a visible shock wave rushed out toward the village, causing all the houses to shake, knocking down those few villagers who were still running around.

The next wave of bombs hit closer in. Then they

started moving toward the village, as if laying a giant carpet of death and total destruction on the jungle floor. Whole trees were uprooted and they flew before the approaching carpet of bombs like twigs in a gale before a storm. A tree landed just in front of the opening of Minh's shelter, and the trunk of that tree acted as a barrier against most of the other flying limbs and debris.

The bomb carpet moved into the village itself and every house was flattened. It marched inexorably through the village, until it was right over Minh's shelter opening, and the tree that had been acting as a barrier exploded into splinters as several bombs fell on it. Minh felt a searing blast of heat, an intense pain, then nothing.

The name of the movie was *Revenge of the Great Hero*. It was a movie about Chinese knights, warriors who possessed almost magical powers in the martial arts. The movies were exceptionally popular with the Vietnamese, and Ernie liked them, not for the action and adventure that thrilled the Vietnamese, but because they were so unbelievable as to be funny. Marty came with him.

At the movie, Ernie and Marty ate dried fruit and salted nuts, and they drank Coke. The cans were too valuable to be given out, so the Coke was poured into plastic sandwich bags. The bag was then twisted shut and sealed around a straw with a rubber band. In order to drink it, one had to hold the bag carefully in hand. It was a little like holding a piece of cold liver.

The soundtrack of the movie was in one Chinese dialect, while another dialect was written in subtitles on the screen. The movie was also subtitled in Vietnamese, French, and English, so that the screen was half covered with words. Despite that, it was great fun, and Ernie booed and hissed when the villains appeared, and cheered lustily for the heroes, and he enjoyed immensely the hours away from the war.

After the movie, he took Marty to his apartment because he had promised to cook her dinner.

Marty was sitting in a wicker chair on the terrace, nursing a gin-and-tonic. There was a glass dining table on the terrace, and the table was already set for two. Around the edge of the terrace was a brick planter, providing soil for a well-maintained hedgerow. Large urns served the same purpose with regard to flowers, so that the rooftop terrace became a lovely, and very private, garden.

Marty could smell the garlic and the wine and the hot butter as Ernie worked in his kitchen. She held her glass aloft.

"Ah, 'tis the burden of the Occidental to come to this accursed land and civilize the heathen. And I intend to start with women's rights. Perhaps I should sell tickets to the Vietnamese women so they can see a man cooking in the house," she suggested.

"Not if you want to eat," Ernie replied good-naturedly.

"Tell me, what is that perfectly heavenly smell?"

"Steak, with *champignons de* Paris," Ernie said. "Only, perhaps I should say *champignons de* Saigon. In truth, I don't know where the mushrooms came from, but they were plump and tender and they will do."

Ernie brought two plates out onto the terrrace. Each plate held a large, steaming steak, smothered in mushrooms. He set the plates down. "With this, I thought we would have an amusing little red wine, not elegant, but adequate." He poured the wine. *"Bon appétit,"* he said.

They ate quietly for a few moments. Then Marty sighed.

"Are we dinosaurs, Ernie? Are we anachronisms, you and I?"

Ernie smiled. "I don't know," he said. "Why would you ask?"

"My editor," Marty said. "He wants me to change the tone and tint of my stories to, and I quote, 'get more with the times,' unquote. It seems my stories are too sympathetic to the fighting man."

"I know what you mean," Ernie said. "The mood of the country — or perhaps I should say the mood of the country's press — is becoming more and more antiwar. Heroic pieces aren't in. They want human-interest pieces."

"Yeah, as long as the human interest shows the U.S. in a bad light," Marty said. "I can't do that, Ernie. I don't know, maybe I've been over here too long . . . with these boys too long. My God, I'm as much against war as anyone. You can't see these kids get blown away day after day without having some feeling about it. But I'm not going to stab them in the back by saying that what they are doing is senseless."

"I know," Ernie said. He smiled. "But not to worry. There are enough red-hot journalists over here after their own Pulitzer that I've no doubt your editor and mine will get what they want, and leave us in peace. In the meantime I will continue to write what I see and feel."

"That's what I said — you're a dinosaur." Marty laughed.

"Like you?"

"Like me," Marty said. "The last two of an extinct species."

Ernie smiled. "Well, you're a girl dinosaur and I'm a boy dinosaur. Maybe we could do something about preserving the species."

"God, I hope not!" Marty said, laughing, and spewing wine.

"Oh," Ernie said, his disappointment showing.

"On the other hand," Marty said, looking at him with eyes that had suddenly grown smoky, "if there are any dinosaurs lurking about, hiding behind curtains and that sort of thing, we might give a demonstration."

"Yeah," Ernie said, refilling her glass. "That's just what I had in mind."

Francis Poindexter woke up to an icy blast of wind. He was unprepared for the cold and he looked around the cabin in some confusion. A nurse walked by.

"What is it?" Francis asked. "What's going on?"

The nurse smiled at him. "Look out your window, soldier," she said. "We are on the ground in Washington, D.C. Welcome to the good old U.S.A."

"I'll be a son of a bitch," Francis said.

"Okay, listen up!" someone shouted, speaking

through a bullhorn from the back of the plane. "Walking wounded, there are buses for you. Officers and top three grades first, then the rest of you. Step quickly, gentlemen, it's cold and we're freezing our stretcher cases."

There weren't that many officers and top three grades, so it quickly became Francis's time to leave. He shuffled through the plane, looking down at the stretcher cases on either side. He saw the boy who had been drinking the root beer. The boy was looking through the window at the lights outside, his eyes dull, his face expressionless.

*Yeah*, Francis thought. *I know what you mean. I hadn't planned to come back this way either.*

"This way, fellas," an airman with a clipboard directed. He was standing by the steps of a blue air force bus. Francis got on, then sat down and waited as the others shuffled onto the bus and took their seats.

"Well," someone said, "we're here."

"Yeah," another said dryly. "Where's the band?"

"Forget the fuckin' band," a third put in. "Where's the bar? I just want to get drunk. I want to get drunk and stay that way for the rest of my life."

"Really," another agreed.

The driver of the bus got on then, followed by the airman with the clipboard. The airman with the clipboard sat on the corner of the front right seat.

"Okay," he said to the driver. "We can go. Gate six."

"Gate six?"

"Yeah, around back."

"What for?" the driver asked. "That's the long way around."

"The captain says there's demonstrators out front."

"Shit! We don't mind a little welcome home," someone said.

"Not that kind of demonstrators," the airman with the clipboard said. "These demonstrators throw bricks at wounded veterans."

"What?"

"What can I tell you?" the airman with the clipboard said. "It's an asshole world."

# Chapter Twelve

Sergeant Mills was dead. He was sitting beside Sergeant Two Bears, eating ham and beans, talking about the '65 Impala he had bought just before he left the States. It had only fifteen thousand miles on it and he got a real good deal. His brother was keeping it, and if it had more than seventeen thousand miles by the time he got back, he was going to kick his brother's ass. It was right after he said that that a sniper's round hit him between the eyes and, with the hydrostatic action of the brain matter, blew out the back of his head.

Preacher was next. He was a born-again Christian who drove everyone nuts with his proselytizing.

They said McGiver was masturbating. He was on ambush patrol and they found him the next morning with his throat cut and his hand in a death grip around his penis. He'd been sitting out there in the middle of the night, maybe excited by some private fantasy, or maybe just trying to stay awake. For some reason his death disturbed the men more than most, as if they themselves had been caught in such an act.

When Bill Hanlon saw how many men had been killed in Hunter Two Bears's platoon, he figured they'd let him move over. He went to Lieutenant Cox and asked to be transferred to the R&P platoon. Cox disapproved.

"You're too valuable to me," he said. "You've got more experience than anyone else in the platoon. In fact I'm going to make you the platoon sergeant."

"You're promoting me to E-6?"

Cox shook his head. "I would if I could," he said. "But I don't have the authority. I can make you an acting jack, though. You can wear the stripes."

"Never mind," Bill said. "If I can't have the pay, the additional stripe doesn't mean anything. I can be your platoon sergeant just the way I am. Who are you going to give my squad to?"

"Who is the senior spec-four?"

"Wilson, but he's no good. He just got here. He can't find his ass with a map and a compass. How about Yard?"

Yard was PFC Yarborough. Yarborough had been in Vietnam longer than Bill. He had been as high as buck sergeant three or four times, but he kept getting busted. His propensity for running afoul and the name Yarborough made his nickname of "Yardbird" a natural. That had been shortened to Yard.

"You really want him?" Cox asked.

"Yes, sir."

Cox sighed and ran his hand over his closely cropped blond hair.

"All right, you can have him." Cox pointed his finger at Bill. "I'll cut out company orders, making him an acting sergeant. But I'm going to hold you responsible for him."

"I'll look out for him," Bill promised.

"Good, good. Now that I have your confidence, I can tell you that your platoon is about to go out on a major sweep."

"My platoon, sir? Not Sergeant Two Bears's?"

"Your platoon," Cox said. He smiled. "Of course, I will lead it."

"Yes, sir."

"We got a break yesterday," Cox went on. "Sergeant Two Bears's platoon made a body-count recon into that village that the B-52's bombed. On one of the dinks they found papers that identified him as Captain Duong Cao Minh of the People's Army."

"No shit? I didn't think those guys carried I.D. cards around," Bill said.

"Normally, they don't," Cox confirmed. "However, the bastard had just completed a meeting with some NVA people and he had a few documents from the meeting. But the most important thing is, we know where the son of a bitch came from." Cox held up a sheet of paper and waved it in front of Bill's face. "He came from My

Song," he said. "My Song is the headquarters for the V.C. core element. We're going to take that headquarters out," Cox said.

"Lieutenant, the moment they realize we're headed for the ville, they'll haul ass out of there," Bill said.

Cox grinned again. "No, they won't," he said. "Not the way I've got it planned. It's a pretty good gimmick, even if I did work up the plan myself."

When Lieutenant Cox laid out his plan for Bill, Bill had to admit that it was a good one. The plan called for a helicopter-lift company to fly to a landing zone, set down as if the helicopters were discharging American troops, then take off again. Five minutes after the choppers took off, American artillery would concentrate a time-on-target attack, laying down a blanket of artillery shells over the entire area.

If any V.C. were drawn to the landing zone by the helicopters, they would be caught in the artillery barrage, but that was just a secondary effect. The primary effect was to keep the attention of the V.C. averted, while Lieutenant Cox and his platoon approached My Song.

Yard was at point, and the patrol moved out in a single file along a jungle trail, keeping the required five-meter separation. Half an hour later, Yard came jogging back toward them.

"We've got a hut up here," he said.

"Abandoned?" Bill asked.

"Doesn't look like it. It's built on a concrete pad and everything."

"Probably some farmer," Cox said. "We'll skip on around it."

"Lieutenant, if it's built on a concrete pad, it's worth checking out," Bill said.

"All right, we'll check it out," Cox said. He looked at his watch, impatiently. "But don't take too long. I want to hit the ville right after noon when they're all taking their nap."

"If you want, Yard and me can take a squad, check it out, then catch up with you."

"You don't need a whole squad," Cox said. "You and Yard do it alone. Move Silverthorn up to point."

"Okay," Bill agreed.

Bill and Yard waited until the platoon had moved on before they hurried down the trail to the hut. When they reached the hut, they saw someone coming out, carrying an AK-47.

"Shit!" Bill said. "V.C.!"

The V.C. saw them almost as soon as they saw him, and he sprayed a long burst of automatic weapons fire toward them. Bill and Yard dived for cover and returned fire with their M-16's on full automatic.

Their bullets ripped through the walls easily, and after a few moments a white flag fluttered out the door.

*"Chieu hoi!"* someone called from inside.

"Okay, come on out!" Bill called.

The door opened and four men came out, holding their hands over their heads.

"Now what?" Bill asked.

"The big question is: Is that all of them?" Yard

replied. "What if there's someone inside waiting for us to show ourselves?"

Bill laughed. "If there's anyone left inside, he must have the rank," he said. "You can bet your ass no officers are going to come out and make themselves bait."

"Well, what are we going to do?"

"I've got an idea," Bill said. He rose to his knees and called to the four V.C., ordering them to come to him. The four V.C. looked at one another nervously, then started across the clearing toward the tree line where Bill and Yard waited.

"Hand me one of your grenades," Bill said, taking one from his own webbing. He pulled the pin, but kept the handle down.

"What the hell are you going to do?"

"Watch."

When the V.C. got to them, Bill gave one of them the two grenades, putting one in each hand, with the pins already pulled. He then gave instructions to walk back over and toss the grenades into the hut.

"What if he throws them at us?"

"If he looks like he's going to, we'll shoot him," Bill said.

The V.C. tried to resist, but Bill pressed them in his hands. Then, with sweat popping out on his face and his eyes darting about nervously, the V.C. started toward the hut. He got about halfway when there was a shot from inside the hut. The V.C. dropped and the two grenades rolled out of his hands.

"Duck!" Bill said.

The two grenades went off with a roar, though

they were far enough away that there were no injuries.

"All right, it isn't empty," Bill said. "Let's call in napalm. We'll burn the sons of bitches out of there."

One of the three remaining prisoners started yelling. Bill couldn't understand what he was saying, though he did recognize the word *napalm*. Now there was another white flag fluttering from the door.

"Okay, tell the son of a bitch to get out here," Bill said. "Tell him to get away from the building. I'm going to call in napalm."

One more V.C. came out of the building holding up his hands. He walked past the body of his comrade he had just killed. When he reached them, the other three started talking to him. Bill couldn't understand what they were saying, but from the tone of voice it seemed pretty obvious they weren't pleased with him.

"What are we going to do with them?" Yard asked.

"We don't have any choice," Bil' said. "We've got to take them back to the compound."

They heard the angry snarl of a turbine engine then, and looked up to see a chopper flying just above the trees. From the crest on the nose, Bill recognized it as a helicopter from Capitol Flight. He spoke into his PRC-6.

"Capitol Huey that just passed over papa seven tango five, this is Wide Receiver. Do you copy?"

"Yeah, Wide Receiver, Capitol Three, go ahead."

"Capitol Three, I have four victor Charley papa

whiskey, say again, four victor Charley papa whiskey. Can you handle them? Over.''

The Huey turned and started circling back. ''Wide Receiver, do they require medical assistance?''

''Negative.''

''Pop smoke, Wide Receiver.''

''Roger, popping smoke now.'' Bill nodded at Yard, who threw a canister out into the clearing. Green smoke began spewing up.

''Roger green?'' the pilot asked.

''Confirm green,'' Bill replied. Bill knew that early in the war the pilots would sometimes request a certain color smoke. The V.C. who had radios would often set off their own smoke grenade, trying to lure the choppers down. The result would be two plumes of the same color. Now the color was never identified until after it was popped.

The helicopter flared out in the clearing, very near where the body of the dead V.C. lay. Two men jumped out through the side door and, carrying .45 handguns, came for the prisoners.

''Thanks for taking them off my hands,'' Bill said.

''No sweat,'' one of the two G.I.'s said. He had a broad smile. ''I'm a clerk at MACV. This is the closest to action I'm going to get.''

''You call, we haul,'' the other one said. They made a motion with their pistols and the four sullen V.C. walked over to the chopper and climbed in. Almost before they were seated the chopper lifted up, then flew away.

''Okay,'' Bill said. ''Let's catch up with that

doofus-assed Cox and see what the hell he's up to.''

Bill and Yard moved quickly through the jungle toward My Song. About thirty minutes later they heard heavy firing from the village.

"Shit! Cox has taken them right into an ambush!'' Yard said.

"Come on,'' Bill said. "We've got to get there.''

They started jogging toward the village. They didn't run all out, because anybody who suddenly burst from the jungle on a dead run was a sure target for a nervous infantryman, especially someone being led by Lieutenant Cox. Cox was not someone who instilled confidence in his men.

Bill and Yard broke out of the clearing, then stopped dead in their tracks.

"Son of a bitch, Bill, what the hell are they doing?'' Yard asked in shock.

"I . . . I don't know,'' Bill said. "God in heaven, I don't know.''

Old men, women, and children from the village were huddled in a ditch that ran just outside the edge of the village. On the berm looking down into the ditch stood about ten men from Cox's platoon. They, and Lieutenant Cox, were firing down into the ditch. Heads were exploding under the crash of bullets.

"Silverthorn,'' Bill said, seeing Silverthorn and the rest of the platoon standing in a group about fifty yards away from where the killing was taking place. Bill pointed to the killing. "What is this? What's this all about?''

"You ask me, that doofus son of a bitch has

gone crazy," Silverthorn said. "When we come in here awhile ago we didn't find one V.C. Not one weapon . . . nothing. So Cox, he just started rounding up the villagers and . . . well . . . you see what he's doing."

"Didn't you try to stop him?"

"He's the lieutenant," Silverthorn said. "I got no right to say anything to him. Besides, there was something about him . . . something in his eyes . . . I'll be honest with you, Sergeant, I want to just stay the fuck away from him."

"Over here!" Cox called. "Get that bunch over here down in the ditch!"

Two or three men herded another bunch of villagers down into the ditch. The villagers knew what was going on. They had seen their neighbors killed and they knew they were next. They went stoically to their doom.

There was no screaming. Bill couldn't believe how quiet they were. It was like some sort of bad dream, where everything was in very, very slow motion, and all sound was muffled.

"Som'bitch! Did you see that?" someone shouted, laughing. "I shot the nipple right off that bitch!"

Bill couldn't even hear the gunfire.

"You got shot in the pecker?" Francis asked.

"No," answered the young red-haired soldier who was in the bed next to Francis. "I didn't really get shot in the pecker. I just tell the women that."

"Why?"

" 'Cause ol' Conally there is such a cocksman he

doesn't want the women bothering him," someone else said.

"Just the opposite," the redhead said. "See, I've got this plan all worked out. I tell them I got shot in the pecker and I'm afraid it won't work anymore. The next thing you know, she's got her hand under the blanket. It's as good as a steam and cream on Plantation Row."

"Shit! There's got to be something better than that," Francis said. "I heard we can get an overnight pass out of here if the doc says it's okay."

"Yeah," Conally answered. "If that's what you want."

"Well, he said it was okay, and I'm going out tonight."

One of the others giggled. "Sounds like a prison break. Hey, pass it down — Poindexter's going over the wall tonight."

"Poindexter's going over the wall tonight," someone else said.

"Anyone got any hot tips?"

No one answered.

"Well, come on, surely there's something to do in Washington. This is a big city," Francis said.

"You ever see *West Side Story?*" Conally asked.

"Yeah. Why?"

"You remember that song where they said everything's all right if you're all white in America?"

"Yeah."

"We got our own song. 'Everything's all right if you're all *there* in Washington.' Most of us here in the pit . . . we don't get into town much."

Conally had a leg missing. Everyone in the ward,

called The Pit by the men, had at least one limb missing; many of them were missing two, and a few, including the young soldier Francis had seen drinking root beer, had three missing.

"Listen, we could get you a wheelchair. I'll push you around," Francis said. "What do you say?"

Conally looked at Francis for a long moment. Then he smiled.

"All right," he said. "You're still such a fuckin' babe in the woods, I guess I better go with you to keep you out of trouble."

The first problem came when they tried to get a cab. Francis flagged a taxi, and when he stopped, Francis opened the back door and started to help Conally in.

"Jeez!" the cabdriver said. "Don't the government have special transportation for you guys? I mean, it takes you so long to get in and out that I lose fares."

"Start your goddamned meter," Francis said.

"Don't worry, I will," the cabdriver said, pushing the flag down.

Conally broke into a sweat getting into the cab, but, with Francis's help, he managed to do it.

"How about putting the wheelchair in the trunk?" Francis asked.

"That'll cost you just like a piece of luggage," the driver said, getting out of the car.

"Just do it," Francis said. With a sigh of disgust, Francis got in beside Conally. Conally looked over at him and, seeing the expression of anger on his face, laughed.

"What's so funny?"

"I was just thinking," Conally said. "You can't

go around pissing people off like you used to.''

"Why the hell not?''

"What happens if you push them into a fight? I'm sure not going to be any help to you. You ever see a one-legged man in an ass-kicking contest?''

Francis frowned at him for a moment. Then the humor of the situation hit him and he laughed out loud. By the time the driver got back into the car, he was laughing so hard that tears were rolling down his face.

"What's so funny?'' the driver asked.

"Nothing,'' Francis said. "Listen, I appreciate you picking us up. I know it's inconvenient.''

"Yeah, well . . .'' the driver said, hemming and hawing now. It was eaiser for him to deal with Francis when Francis was being bellicose. "Always glad to help a wounded vet,'' he said.

"Especially this one,'' Francis said, pointing to Conally. "He got shot right in the pecker, and he doesn't know if it will work anymore. We're going to try and find a girl who'll test it out for him.''

Conally laughed.

"No shit?'' the driver asked.

"You wouldn't know where we might find some willing girl to do her duty to her country, do you?''

The driver picked up a chewed, unlit stogie from his ashtray, then stabbed it in his mouth. He smiled around the edge of it.

"Well, now, it just so happens that I do,'' he said. "It might cost you a few dollars, but she's worth it. Believe me. She's young, blonde, clean, and sexy.''

"What do you think, Conally? You want to try?'' Francis asked.

"Well, what do you know?'' Conally said. "I

can feel it twitching around down there, just thinking about it. By Jove, I do believe it's going to work. Let's go.''

"You got it," the driver said. He put the flag back down, then pulled out into the traffic.

"How much you think it's going to cost?" Conally asked.

"What the hell difference does it make?" Francis answered. "We've already given an arm and a leg.''

# Chapter Thirteen

Hunter handed Bill a beer. Bill tapped the top with the church key, punched it open, then passed the opener back to Hunter Two Bears. Hunter opened his own while Bill sucked down the warm suds.

"Okay," Hunter said. "I want to know what happened."

"What do you mean, what happened?" Bill answered defensively.

"Goddammit! I know something happened out there today." Hunter said. "What happened? What did you guys run into?"

"Has anyone said anything?"

"No."

"No, they haven't and they won't," Bill said. "They're afraid of what Lieutenant Cox and the others might do."

"What others?" Hunter wanted to know.

"The others who were with him. The ones who went along with it."

"Goddammit!" Hunter roared. "Hanlon, you better tell me what the fuck went on out there."

Bill took another long, Adam's-apple-bobbing swallow of his beer. "You wouldn't believe me," he said finally, speaking so quietly that Hunter could barely hear him.

"Try me."

"You remember what you told me about your great-grandpa or whoever getting killed at Wounded Knee? How it happened? How the soldiers just opened fire?"

"Yes."

"The army hasn't learned much since then," Bill said.

"What are you talking about?" Hunter asked, but even as he asked the question he felt chills pass over him. He knew what Bill was talking about.

"Murder, Hunter. Cox and about ten or fifteen of his bunch lined up all the people from that little village and shot them down. They killed little babies who couldn't even walk, children, mothers with babies suckin' on the breast, old women, and old men. They killed them all. They shot them down like they were cutting wheat." Bill laughed, though it was more like a grunt than a laugh. "Would you believe they gave some of the kids C's before they killed them? One of the kids just stood there, eating . . ." — Bill's voice broke — ". . . eating that fuckin' scrambled eggs and ham while he waited for them to shoot him. By the time they got through, there were more than a hundred killed.''

Hunter felt a hollowness in the pit of his stomach and a weakness in his knees. He squeezed his can so tightly that it collapsed and beer squirted from the top.

''Are you going to tell the colonel?'' Hunter wanted to know.

''No, I'm not.''

''Why not?''

''It would be my word against the lieutenant's,'' Bill said.

''No, it wouldn't. You've got a dozen witnesses.''

''Hunter, the platoon was split exactly in half. Half the men did it, and half the men didn't. Now, the ones who didn't participate didn't have the stomach for killing civilians. On the other hand, I can't see them turning in their buddies either, not for what they see as a bunch of dead dinks.''

''I see,'' Hunter said.

''The only thing we can do is try and live with it,'' Bill said. He took a thoughtful drink of his beer. ''Some of us are going to find that harder than others,'' he added.

''This way,'' Phat called to the fifteen or so men who remained from his company. Phat, now a veteran of five years' fighting, was a sergeant, the highest-ranking member of the original My Song Company. After Captain Minh was killed, the Central Committee assigned another officer, a lieutenant, to the My Song Company. But he hadn't been with them long, and he was a North

Vietnamese regular, so Phat was the one with the most experience. The My Song Company had been out on a sortie when the Americans came to the village. When Phat and the others returned to find everyone dead and the village burned, the NVA lieutenant decided it was time to move on.

Phat and the others felt no particular sorrow over what had happened in the village. The My Song Company had been controlling the villagers by terror tactics anyway. The Americans didn't understand that tactic — they just came in and blew everyone away. It was a waste . . . but it wasn't particularly a tragedy.

The lieutenant had been following a trail to the east, to sanctuary on the Cambodian side of the border. But when they crossed a small stream, Phat turned south.

"Sergeant Phat, the lieutenant wants us to cross the border," one of the men said.

"We'll never make it," Phat replied. "The Americans will have soldiers there, blocking us off."

"How could they? They don't know where we are going."

"They know everything," Phat said. "Haven't you figured this out yet? They have airplanes that can see in the dark, see us under the trees. They know where we are going."

Ngo Nhu, the North Vietnamese lieutenant, came back to see what the discussion was about.

"What are you doing, Sergeant Phat?" he hissed. "We have to join our comrades across the border."

"I think not," Phat said. "The Americans will

be waiting for us. We must work our way south."

"We are going across the border!" Ngo Nhu ordered.

Phat pointed his AK-47 at the NVA lieutenant.

"Lieutenant Nhu, if you wish to cross the border, you go ahead. I am going south here."

"Fool! I will report you to the Central Committee. You will be shot!"

"If you try to cross the border, you won't live long enough to talk to the Central Committee," Phat said.

"We shall see about that," Nhu replied. He looked at the others. "Come with me," he ordered.

"I choose to stay with Sergeant Phat," one of the others said, and three more agreed with him. The remaining men, about ten, went with the lieutenant, and they crossed the stream, heading east.

"I will report this mutiny," Nhu called back angrily.

Phat watched Nhu and the others as they crossed the stream and started across the rice paddies for the hills beyond.

"Phat, let us go quickly," said one of those who stayed with him.

"Wait," Phat said. He held up his hand. "Let's see if they make it."

Phat and his four companions hid behind the stream bank and watched. Nhu and his followers moved out onto the rice paddy, running quickly along one of the dikes.

Suddenly two helicopters appeared from behind and over Phat's head. They were flying fast and low, and they zipped by overhead, totally unaware of Phat's existence. They started for Nhu and his men.

Phat raised up and fired at the two helicopters. The others joined with him and they were rewarded for their efforts by the sight of black smoke streaming back from the engine of one of the helicopters.

Both helicopters opened fire on Nhu and his men, and Phat saw Nhu and the others dive off the dike and splash down into the flooded paddy. Automatic-weapons fire coming from the vegetation across the paddy told Phat that he was correct in his belief that the Americans would be waiting in a blocking position. As Phat stared across the paddy, he saw scores of American soldiers coming out of the trees, moving toward Nhu and his men.

The helicopter Phat had hit turned and started down toward the paddy to make an emergency landing. Phat fired again at the helicopter, and he saw the front windshield of the ship fill with holes as his bullets sprayed into it. The helicopter, which had been coming down in a smooth descent, suddenly lurched and fell over on its side. It crashed hard, then exploded into a great, greasy ball of flame.

"Son of a bitch!" Phat heard one of the American infantrymen shout. "Lookit that!"

The remaining helicopter made another pass over Nhu and his few remaining men. Then the Americans closed with them. The fighting was short and furious. Then it stopped. Nhu, and every man who had started across the rice paddy with him, lay dead.

"Let's go," Phat said quietly. He started downstream, keeping under the trees so he wouldn't be detected by any aircraft that might be flying over them.

"Sergeant Phat, you'll be in command now," one of the others said. "Nhu was the last officer in the province."

"Yes," Phat said. "I know."

Hunter Two Bears went TDY to a radio-relay station to help set up a perimeter of defense. He was gone for seven days, and when he came back he learned that Bill Hanlon had transferred to another line unit. He was certain that Bill wouldn't have transferred if Cox had only moved him to his platoon. Angry, he went to Cox to find out why he had let Hanlon go.

"We're better off without him," Cox said. "He was nothing but a troublemaker anyway."

"He was the best goddamned soldier in this company," Hunter said. "Company, hell! He was the best in the battalion."

"Perhaps I knew him a little better than you," Cox said. "I saw him differently."

"That's bullshit and you know it," Hunter said. "You transferred him because you were afraid of him. Well, that's the real funny part of it, Lieutenant. You didn't have to be afraid of him, because he wasn't going to say anything. The one you have to be afraid of is me."

Lieutenant Cox's eyes narrowed and turned to ice. "I'm sure I have no idea what you are talking about," Cox said.

"In a pig's ass you don't know. You think

you're going to be able to keep what you did at My Song a secret? My God, Lieutenant, you wasted over a hundred civilians.''

''Sergeant Two Bears, I don't know what you know . . . or what you think you know, but I rendered a complete report on the My Song mission. It was a good operation and I'm proud of it. In fact, I have it on very good authority that I will be getting the 'V' device for my Bronze Star.''

''You make me sick,'' Hunter said.

''Sergeant, one more word out of you and I'll have you up on charges.''

''You won't do shit, Lieutenant,'' Hunter said. ''You don't want anyone to start poking around My Song.''

Cox looked at Hunter for a long moment. Then he smiled, a slow, evil smile. ''It might interest you to know that Sergeant Hanlon is up for the same award,'' he said. ''I'm sure you wouldn't want to do anything that would screw things up for your friend. Especially since he would wind up facing charges as well.''

''Why would he face charges? He didn't have anything to do with it.''

''He was there, Sergeant. He was there and he saw what happened. He's been back over a week, but he's made no report of any kind. By his silence, he has become a co-defendant, as it were.''

''Then you admit you did it?'' Hunter asked.

''No, Sergeant, I admit no such thing,'' Cox said. ''I was just pointing out a few fallacies in what you advanced as your plan of action, that's all. Now, if there's nothing else?''

Hunter looked at Cox and he squeezed his hands into such tight fists that his knuckles turned white. Oh, how he would love to bust the lieutenant right in the mouth.

Dear Billy,

You will forgive your mother for calling you Billy, won't you? I guess it's not the name you're known by, by all of your buddies, but you will always be Billy to me.

The most awful thing happened last night. You remember Jim Freeman, the boy who had the real pretty red car? The one with the special paint job? He was a friend of yours in school, I think. Anyway, last night he had a wreck and was killed. They say he had been drinking. He was driving over one hundred miles an hour and he hit the back end of a big trailer truck. He was going so fast that he knocked the rear wheels right out from under the trailer and the trailer just sort of collapsed on him and crushed him under the car.

Well, enough of that. You'll be pleased to know that I've been promoted. Yep, I am now a full-fledged associate. We'll have to have a little party to celebrate when you come back home.

Billy, I'm having a hard time explaining to everybody why you went back to Vietnam. They all think you're crazy. Maybe what's making it so hard for me is that I also think it was a crazy thing to do. I know you were having a difficult time in school, but honey, that didn't mean you had to go back in the army. I wish you would have come to talk to me about it.

Nobody likes this war. Everyone is demonstrating against it all the time. Why, would you believe that last week some protesters or somebody actually threw bricks at the wounded as they were coming back to the States?

Speaking of wounded, you got a postcard from somebody named Francis Poindexter. He's in the hospital in Washington, D.C., and he wants you to come up and see him. From the sound of the card, he must not know that you went back.

Be careful, Billy. Write soon.

Love,
Mother

"What'll we do with his bunk? You want me to turn it in, or what?"

"No sense in that. There'll be a replacement in pretty soon. Then we'd just have to draw another one. Why don't you stockade it?"

"Okay. Listen, I'm going to trade mattresses with him, if that's all right."

"Yeah, sure, go ahead. He sure as hell won't mind."

"What do you want to do about his personals?"

"Anything there that shouldn't be?"

"He had some rubbers in his billfold."

"Take 'em out. Anything else? Any whore's letters, fuck books — anything like that?"

"No."

"Okay, leave the rest. Someone from supply will inventory 'em and take care of 'em."

"It was a damned shame. He just got here."

"No, he didn't. He'd been in-country a long time. He just transferred over here, that's all. He knew what to expect."

"He was a strange one, really kept to himself."

"Yeah. I asked him about where he'd been, what he'd done, but he never would talk about it. He said something strange once."

"What was that?"

"He said he couldn't hear them scream. If he could hear them scream, he would be all right."

"Hear who scream?"

"Beat's the shit out of me."

"Mail call!" someone called from the front of the tent. "Anderson!"

"Yeah."

"Baker."

"Right here."

"Lindell." The clerk sniffed Lindell's letter, then let out a long sigh. "Son of a bitch, Lindell, every time I deliver a letter to you, my hands smell like I been in a French whorehouse."

"That's the closest your hands ever get to that smell, my man," Lindell said. The others laughed.

"Hanlon," the clerk called.

There was silence in the squad tent.

"Sergeant Bill Hanlon."

"He got hit on ambush last night."

"Where is he? First Field?" the mail clerk asked. "I gotta know where to forward the letter."

"Send it back."

"Send it back? What do you mean, send it back?"

"Hanlon's dead."

# Chapter Fourteen

Ernie was sitting at a table on the veranda of the Continental Hotel. He would have preferred a table right near the entrance, but it was occupied by a man Ernie recognized as the Minister of Imports. The minister was reading a newspaper, and the fat, sausagelike fingers of both his hands were adorned with diamond rings. Rolls of flesh from his thick neck lay in layers across the silk collar of his expensive suit.

The conversations being conducted in the Continental were in French, Vietnamese, and Chinese. Ernie couldn't follow the Chinese, but the French and Vietnamese conversations dealt with things as diverse as the price of rubber on the international market to a ballet being performed in Cholon. No one was talking about the war, and Ernie saw a perfect example of something that he frequently tried to point out to other Americans, but was unable to make them grasp. The stratum of society represented by the people with whom Americans normally had contact was totally isolated from the mainstream of the Vietnamese people. It curled and seeped through the population like an oil slick in water, moving with the current, seemingly a part of the whole, but never actually emulsifying.

It was early afternoon and Ernie was drinking a "33" beer. He had an appointment with Colonel Craig Pardee, the MACV P.I.O. officer. Colonel Pardee wanted to know why very few of his carefully worded P.I.O. "Action Reports" showed up in Ernie's stories. Pardee was very proud of his "Action Reports," and he went to great lengths to make the reports exciting.

Colonel Pardee arrived fifteen minutes late. He was wearing khakis and a garrison cap, complete with "scrambled eggs" on the bill. He was wearing aviator sunglasses, though Ernie noticed he wasn't wearing wings. Colonel Pardee's chest was adorned with what the G.I.'s called the "Vietnam basic load" of ribbons. There were two Vietnam service medals, the red-and-yellow ribbon awarded by the government of Vietnam, and green-and-white ribbon awarded by the United States. The green, white, brown, and blue National Defense ribbon completed the bottom row. The next row started with the green Army Commendation, and the red Bronze Star for Service award. He was also wearing the blue-and-gold Air Medal, earned by frequent flights to the beaches of Vung Tau. There were no "V's" on any of the medals, and there was no C.I.B., though there were crossed rifles on the left collar point, and a silver leaf on the right. Colonel Pardee, who had never heard a shot fired in anger, was the absolute model of the straphanger, also sometimes referred to as the REMF, of rear-area motherfucker.

"Ah, Mr. Chapel," Colonel Pardee said, weaving his way through the tables to get to Ernie. He was carrying a briefcase and he set it on the green-and-white terrazzo floor beside his chair. "I'm sorry to keep you waiting, but duty doth occasionally detain."

"You do have a way with words, Colonel," Ernie said dryly.

"Yes, that is a nice turn of phrase, don't you think?"

A white-jacketed waiter appeared.

"I'll have a gin-ton," Colonel Pardee ordered. "You, Mr. Chapel?"

"I'm fine," Ernie said, indicating that his beer was practically full. Ernie was a little surprised that Colonel Pardee had ordered a drink in the middle of the day. Particularly since the colonel was on duty.

"I once read," the colonel said, "that England gave three gifts to civilization: the most expressive language, rare roast beef, and gin-and-tonic. The Frogs might argue over the language, the Chinks over the roast beef, but no one will dispute the medicinal value of a gin-and-tonic, well mixed." The waiter returned and Colonel Pardee held his glass out to Ernie. "Cheers," he said.

Ernie, without replying, raised his glass of beer.

"Now," Colonel Pardee said, putting his glass

down and opening his briefcase. "I want you to look at some of the action reports I've prepared for release this week and see if there isn't one you might be able to use." He handed a sheaf of papers across the table to Ernie.

The crashing glass caused everyone in the bar to duck from the flying splinters. A few jagged pieces of the mirror hung in the frame, and their daggerlike slivers reflected in the face of Hunter Two Bears, twisted in rage.

A bar girl, her eyes cobra-lidded and darkly painted, moved over to Hunter.

"What's the matta you? Why you do this?" she asked, pointing to the shattered glass on the floor.

"He's dead," Hunter said. "He's dead and it's Cox's fault."

"Maybe you buy me drink you feel better," the girl suggested.

Hunter pounded his fist on the bar. "I should've killed the son of a bitch," he said.

The girl, deciding that the tall, swarthy G.I. wasn't fit company, made a face.

"You dinky-dau, G.I.," she said. "You crazy."

"Get the fuck away from me!" Hunter said. He took another drink.

"Hey, fella," a master sergeant called. The master sergeant was in khakis, his overseas cap neatly tucked into his belt. "I don't know how you do it in the field, but here we don't talk like that around ladies."

Hunter stared at the master sergeant. He didn't say a word but his eyes, picking up the red lights behind the bar, flashed angrily. A few people standing nearby almost expected to see laser beams shooting from his eyes. The master sergeant turned and walked away quickly.

Hunter killed his drink, then walked outside. He was in front of Maxim's Bar, and he stood at the sandbag barricade to let his eyes adjust to the bright, afternoon light.

Hunter was wearing fatigues, not the stifling starched jungle fatigues of the Saigon Warriors, but the soiled fatigues of a man who had worn them in combat. The black stripes pinned to his collar were barerly visible, his name tag and the U.S. Army flash were unreadable, and he was wearing no shoulder patch. He had on a web belt and empty holster. He was carrying a pistol in his trousers leg pocket. Because he wore a helmet in the field, he was without a hat.

An M.P. Jeep slowed in front of the bar. "Get a hat, soldier," one of the M.P.'s called.

Technically, Hunter was AWOL. He didn't want to be picked up by the M.P.'s for any infraction, because it would take very little to find out his status. In fact, word might already have gone out.

Hunter stepped back inside the bar. He saw a hat lying on a table, so he took it. It had a small, black, First Cavalry pin on it. Hunter wasn't a member of the First Cavalry but it made no difference to him. He put it on, then went back out front and flagged down a cyclo.

"I grant you, they are well-written pieces," Ernie was saying. "But surely, Colonel, you can understand my position. It's a matter of job preservation. If I start using generic material, my editors are likely to wonder why they're paying to have me over here in the first place."

"I understand all that, but —" The colonel's rebuttal was interrupted by a loud, barking call from a rather scruffy-looking soldier who was standing just at the entrance to the Continental's veranda.

"Chapel! Chapel, these sons of bitches won't let me in to see you, so you get your ass out here!"

Ernie looked around toward the disturbance and was surprised to see SFC Hunter Two Bears.

"Hunter! What are you doing here?"

"I came to see you, you feather-merchant civilian asshole. But these slope-headed bastards won't let me come in 'cause I'm not properly dressed."

"See here, Sergeant," Colonel Pardee said, starting toward Hunter.

"I'll handle this, Colonel," Ernie said quickly.

"No, by God, I'll handle it," Pardee said. "This man is a disgrace to the uniform."

"He's drunk, Colonel," Ernie said. "He doesn't know what he's doing."

"All the more reason to get him off the streets."

"What are you coming over here for, straphanger?" Hunter asked.

"What? What did you call me?"

"Oh, excuse me, *Sir*," Hunter said. "I meant, what are you coming over here for, straphanger, *Sir*?"

"Sergeant, I don't know who you are, or where you came from, but I hope this little episode has been enjoyable for you. I imagine it took you eight or ten years to make those stripes. You are about to lose them all in two minutes.''

"Fuck you, straphanger."

"What did you say?" Colonel Pardee got so red in the face that Ernie thought he was going to have a stroke.

"Hunter, go get us a taxi. I'll be right with you."

"You goddamned right you'll be right with me," Hunter said. "Me and you got some serious talking to do." Hunter staggered back across the sidewalk, then hailed one of the little blue-and-yellow Renault taxicabs. He sat in the backseat and told the driver to wait.

"I'm going to burn that sergeant's ass," Colonel Pardee said.

"Colonel, he's been in the field, he's seen some rough times. Let me calm him down."

"I'm sick and tired of the field troopers coming into Saigon like they have an edict from God," Pardee said. "I won't put up with it."

"Suppose I promise to use your release, as written, in my next story?"

"You're not doing me any favors, you know. That's my job," Pardee said.

"And I'll credit you," Ernie offered.

"You'll credit me with the story?"

"Yes."

Pardee rubbed his chin, then looked toward the taxi. Hunter was leaning his head back on the seat, as if totally unconcerned about what was going on. Pardee sighed. "All right," he said. He pointed at Hunter. "But I better never see that son of a bitch again."

"I'll get him sobered up and cleaned up," Ernie promised.

"Don't change one word."

"Deal," Ernie said. Ernie hurried over to the taxi, gave the driver an address, and then the taxi made a big U-turn against the traffic and started back down Le Loi.

Colonel Pardee walked over to the telephone, then called the provost marshal's office of the Saigon Area Command.

"Yes, this is Colonel Pardee from Military Assistance Command, Vietnam. I would like you to locate and apprehend an SFC for me."

"Apprehend, Colonel?" the voice on the other end asked. "Are you prepared to file charges?"

"Yes, yes, I will file charges," Pardee said.

"What is the nature of the charges?"

"Drunk and disorderly, conduct unbecoming, insubordination, out of uniform, and, I wouldn't doubt, AWOL."

"AWOL charges will have to be filed by the sergeant's command," the provost marshal spokesman said. "What is the sergeant's name?"

For a moment Pardee was stuck. Then he remembered hearing Chapel call the sergeant by name. He also remembered seeing the First Cavalry pin on the sergeant's hat.

"Hunter," he said, smiling. "Sergeant First Class Hunter, from the First Air Cavalry."

"All right, Colonel, we'll get right on it," the provost marshal promised.

Colonel Pardee hung up the phone and returned to his table, where he ordered another drink. Maybe he had promised Chapel he wouldn't do anything, but Chapel was a civilian and this was a matter for the military. If he didn't do his duty, he couldn't live with himself. Civilians just didn't understand anything like that.

"Your gin-ton, Colonel," the waiter said.

"Thank you," Pardee replied. He took a drink, then wiped the back of his hand across his mouth. *Yes, sir,* he thought. *Civilians just wouldn't understand.*

Approximately forty-five minutes later, Hunter Two Bears, showered and in a fresh pair of fatigues supplied by Ernie Chapel, walked out onto Ernie's patio. Ernie had whipped up a pot of chili while Hunter was showering, and now he spooned up a bowl for each of them.

"I'm not sure I can handle that," Hunter said, nodding at the chili.

"Sure you can," Ernie said. "You're not hung over, you're just drunk. You need something to eat, and the spices will sober you up real fast."

"Okay," Hunter said. He sat down and Ernie poured him a cup of coffee. Hunter took a swallow of coffee, then a bite of chili. "Damn," he said. "It really is good."

Both men were silent for several moments. Then, after the food was consumed and the bowls carried back into the kitchen, Ernie came back onto the patio and poured another cup of coffee for each of them.

"You want to tell me about it?" Ernie asked finally.

"Bill Hanlon's dead," Hunter said.

"I'm sorry to hear that. I know you liked him."

"He was . . . he was like a little brother," Hunter said. "I mean, he was a feisty little son of a bitch. I don't know why I liked him. But I did."

"Is that why you went AWOL?"

"Yeah. No. I mean, there's more to it than that. Ernie, I'm going to tell you a story that you won't believe. But believe it. Every word of it is true."

"I'm listening," Ernie said.

Hunter took a sip of coffee, then in slow, quiet words told Ernie the story of My Song. When he was finished with the story there was a long moment of silence. Finally, Ernie spoke again.

"Hunter, are you telling me this because you want me to print it? Because if you are, you know I'll have to have half a dozen verifications before my editor will even come close to it."

"I know, I know," Hunter said, waving his hand. He sighed. "To be honest, Ernie, I don't know why the hell I told you. I guess I just had to have someone to talk to, that's all. I'm not going to go off and blow myself away the way Bill Hanlon did."

"Blow himself away? What do you mean?"

"He couldn't stay with the company anymore," Hunter said. "So he transferred out. He got killed the first night he went on ambush patrol."

"Yeah, but that could happen to anyone," Ernie said.

"Not this way. I went over to find out about it. You know what they told me?"

Ernie shook his head.

"When the V.C. hit, Bill stood up. He just stood up and started walking out across that rice paddy, shooting his M-16 from his hip. He just walked right toward them, like he was on parade.''

Ernie remembered his own night on ambush patrol. He remembered how terrifying it had been when the V.C. hit . . . how he had made himself as small as possible while he was loading magazines for Pepper. He thought of what it must have been like for Bill to just stand up and walk toward the V.C.

"You're right," he said. "He blew himself away."

"He couldn't live with what he saw," Hunter said. Hunter sighed. "And I can understand it, 'cause I'm having a hell of a time living with what I know.''

"I hope you aren't planning on doing anything like that," Ernie said.

"No, I'm not. I didn't have anything to do with it. . . . I'm not the one who should be blown away. Neither was Bill." Hunter stood up and rubbed the back of his hand across his mouth. "Listen, I've got to get on back to An Loi," he said. "The last courier flight leaves in about an hour, and I need to be on it. If I can get back tonight, I'll be okay. Thanks for sobering me up, feeding me, and listening to me.''

"Sure," Ernie said. "Listen, are you all right?"

"Yeah, I am now," Hunter said.

"That's an incredible story you told me. Would you like me to look into it more — try and come up with the verifications so I can write it?"

"No, that's all right," Hunter said. He smiled, though the smile barely reached his eyes. "Just talkin' to you about it was good enough. I feel a lot better now, really I do.''

"Hunter?''

"Yeah?''

"Keep your head down, okay?''

"You got it.''


As Hunter stood on the curb waiting for a cab, a Jeep with two M.P.'s pulled up beside him. Hunter looked them.

"Excuse me,'' one of the M.P.'s said. He read the name tags on the shirt . . . Chapel on one side, Correspondent on the other. "Mr Chapel?''

For a second Hunter almost corrected him. Then he remembered he was wearing Chapel's correspondent uniform.

"Yes?'' Hunter asked.

"We're looking for a sergeant first class, a man named Hunter. He's with the First Cav.''

"You'd know him if you saw him,'' the other M.P. said. "He's a big man, and according to the word we got, he's so drunk he can barely stand.''

"What did he do?'' Hunter asked.

"He cussed out Colonel Pardee,'' the first M.P. said.

Hunter chuckled. If they were looking for an SFC Hunter from the First Air Cavalry, there was no way they could even trace it back to him. "I met Colonel Pardee,'' Hunter said. "If you ask me, they should give this Sergeant Hunter a medal.'' Hunter saw a taxi and flagged it down. "Excuse me, gentlemen,'' he said. "I have a flight to catch.''

# Chapter Fifteen

Sergeant Phat was now Captain Phat. It didn't really mean anything; soldiers of the People's Liberation Army weren't paid a regular salary, they just took what they needed. The fact that Phat was already in charge meant that he could take what he needed anyway.

Some thought it would mean something after the victory. After the victory the officers and leaders of the liberation movement would be the officers and leaders of the new army and new government. They would have the finest villes in Saigon or Vung Tau. They would have the Mercedeses and the Fords . . . if they survived.

When Phat first joined the liberation army he sometimes dreamed of the glory and power that would be his after victory. Then he saw so many of his comrades fall around him that his goal became much more modest. He began to dream only of surviving the war. Then, even more modestly, he hoped to survive from day to day. He no longer even thought about that. He learned sometime ago that if he would consider himself already dead, nothing could bother him. He was now the walking dead, with ho hopes, no ambitions, no loves or passions, no hunger or feelings, and no fear.

It was because Phat had no fear of the present and no hope for the future that he did not flinch when orders came down to lead a sapper team through the wire at An Loi. It was a suicide mission, and all who took it understood that. There had always been suicide missions during times of war, most notably the suicide missions of the Kamikaze pilots during World War II. The Kamikaze pilots were ennobled by their status, elevated almost to the rank of gods.

There was no such elevation with Phat or the other members of his sapper team. In their minds they were already dead anyway, and beyond such things as glory, patriotism, or honor. They undertook the assignment with the same calmness they showed when ordered to unload a cart of rice.

It was just before dawn. There were three men at bunker number five, a PFC, a spec-four and a spec-five. The spec-five was in charge, and they were "blasting" pot. That was to say, one man would inhale a mouthful of smoke, then blow it through a gun barrel into the mouth of another. This had the effect of making a hit more concentrated, thus producing a more intense high.

"Oh, wow, far out!" the PFC said. The gun barrel they were using was the barrel of his riot shotgun. The bunker was equipped with an M-60 machine gun, known as a "pig," an M-16, and a twelve-gauge shotgun. The shotgun would be effective only at close range, so they felt secure in breaking it down to use it for blasting. "Sheeeit!" the PFC shouted. Then he laughed.

"Goddammit! Keep it down!" the spec-five warned. "You want the N.C.O.I.C. to come snoopin' around?"

"Don't worry 'bout that motherfucker, man. He ain't gonna come outta his bunker all night long. That man's cuttin' some z's, man."

"What was that?" the spec-four asked.

"What was what?"

"That sound. I heard a . . . a pinging sound."

"A ping? Like someone cutting through the wire?" the PFC asked.

"Yeah, man," the spec-four said. "Like someone cutting through the wire."

The PFC laughed. The PFC had been busted from spec-five, and he was an old hand in Vietnam. The spec-four was new.

"I used to hear that kinda shit all the time myself," the PFC said. "The first few times you come out on the wire, man, you spend the whole night thinkin' Charlie's sneakin' up on your ass. Everything you hear, you think it's Charlie. There ain't nothin' out there. Come on, give me another blast."

The spec-four took a deep drag, then got ready. The PFC put the end of the gun barrel in his mouth and waited. The smoke hit his lungs at about the same time the knife hit his back. When he gasped, the other two thought it was the result of the smoke. By the time he fell forward with a knife in his back, four V.C. were crawling into the bunker. The M-16 was leaning against the corner, the M-60 was pointed away from the compound, and the short-range riot gun was broken down. The spec-five and the spec-four had no means of defense. They were killed before they could make a sound.

Three men who had taken a very early shower in order to beat the rush were heading back for their tent when the machine gun opened up. The M-60 at bunker number five was turned onto the compound and red tracers sprayed out like water from a garden hose. The bullets cut through the tents and smashed into the latrines and showers. The three men who had just stepped out were cut down by the fire.

"Jeez! What's happening?" someone shouted.

"Charlie's through the wire! Charlie's through the wire!"

Hunter started toward the company C.P. There was a hand-cranked siren at the company C.P., and though he was fairly certain that everyone knew they were under attack by now, he thought he should sound it. Also, there was a radio in company headquarters that would allow him to call in support.

A line of green tracer rounds zipped toward him from the company C.P., and he had to dive for the ground. Green meant Charlie. The company C.P. had fallen.

A series of explosions from around the compound let Hunter know that there were sappers at work. The generator went up and all the lights went off. A fuel truck exploded in a great roar, sending a huge ball of fire up into the air.

Hunter headed for the battalion C.P., where he found Colonel Petery crouching behind the sandbag barricade. Petery was wearing his flak jacket and helmet and he had a .45 in his hand.

"How many are there, Sergeant Two Bears?"

"I don't know, sir," Hunter said.

"Sounds like there's an entire regiment."

"Colonel, there's no way an entire regiment could have sneaked through the wire."

"I know, I know. Where's Cox? Why hasn't he answered the phone?"

"He may be dead, Colonel. Charlie has the company C.P."

"Son of a bitch," Petery said. He sighed. "All right, you get back and take charge of your sector. It's probably best not to send any of the other company officers over there. They could get their asses shot off by your own men."

"Yes, sir," Hunter said.

Hunter started back toward his company sector. When he was even with the mess tent, he was fired on by four or five people from the next tent down, the tent where the cooks and bakers lived. He dived into a mud puddle and lay there with the water up to his ears. Had the V.C. taken that tent, or was he being fired on by his own men? He tried to rise up, and another stream of tracers came toward him.

"Who are you?" one of the men shouted. Hunter recognized Casey's voice. Sergeant Casey was the mess sergeant.

"Goddamn it! Casey, don't you think you could've found that out before you started shooting?"

"It's Sergeant Two Bears," Hunter heard one of the cooks say.

"Yes, goddammit! It's me!" Hunter shouted.

"Well, come on, then, we won't shoot," Casey called.

"Damned decent of you," Hunter replied. He got up, brushed some of the mud off, then ran over to the tent. There was still a lot of shooting going on around the compound area.

"We're sorry, Sarge," Casey said when Hunter stepped into the tent, behind the sandbag walls. "We thought you were Charlie."

"You sure you don't want to ask me something . . . like who won the World Series or some shit like that?" Hunter asked disgustedly.

"I told you, we're sorry," Casey said again.

"Yeah. Well, what the hell are you doing shooting anyway? Why aren't you cooking breakfast?"

"Cooking breakfast? Are you crazy? Charlie's come through the wire, goddammit!"

"What the hell difference does that make? Men still gotta eat, and you're trained to cook breakfast while you're being shot at. Besides, right now you're doing just what he wants you to do. The more of our people he can get to shooting, the more chance we have of killing ourselves. You just get over into the mess tent and don't touch a weapon unless he comes right in and helps himself to a cup of coffee."

"Okay, Sarge, if that's what you want."

"Yeah, that's what I want."

Hunter went to the other tents and calmed them down as well, until finally all the shooting was stopped. When things were calm, he put a squad together and led them outside. By now there was a pale streak of light in the east.

Hunter had called all the bunkers, and got a reply from everyone except bunker number five. The first place he took the squad to was number five. He found the three American bodies there, plus the body of the V.C. who had turned the pig onto the compound. He also found the cut in the wire where Charlie came through. He left three men to secure the bunker, then took the rest of the squad toward the company C.P. He put his men out in a semi-circle around the C.P., then waited.

Within fifteen more minutes, the gray light of dawn illuminated the compound and Hunter could see all around. The sappers had done a pretty good job. They took out the generator, fuel truck, three Jeeps, and a supply shed. The fuel truck and the supply shed were still burning. There were three V.C. bodies on the ground. Hunter realized they must have just been caught in the crossfire, because for the first several minutes after the attack there was no aimed fire, just mad shooting.

"What we gonna do, Sarge?" Pepper asked.

"Get a couple of M-79 rounds on the C.P.," Hunter said.

Pepper signaled to the M-79 carriers, and two 40-mm rounds were fired at the C.P. They exploded with a low thump.

"Hey, Charlie!" Hunter shouted. "If you're in there, you better *chieu hoi*, or we're going to burn you out of there. Get the flame-thrower, Pepper.''

Pepper looked at Hunter in surprise. There wasn't a flame-thrower in the company. As far as Pepper knew, there wasn't one in the entire compound.

"Get the flame-thrower. We're going to burn their asses good.''

"No!'' a voice called from inside the C.P. A white flag fluttered from above the sandbags. "No burn.''

"Then come on out of there,'' Hunter called. "Cover them,'' he said to his men.

There was a movement behind the sandbags. Then two people emerged through the pall of smoke. One was a V.C. The other was Lieutenant Cox. The V.C. had a pistol pointing at Lieutenant Cox's head. The V.C. was smiling.

"I am Captain Phat of the People's Liberation Army,'' Phat said. "I am holding your lieutenant as a hostage. I am going to walk out the gate with your lieutenant. Then I will free him. If you try and stop me, I will shoot him.''

"Do what he says, Sergeant Two Bears,'' Cox said in a frightened voice.

"I believe he's bluffing,'' Hunter said. He started walking toward Phat and Cox, holding his M-16 in front of him.

"He's not bluffing, believe me,'' Cox said in a frightened voice.

"Sure he is,'' Hunter said calmly. "Why, he knows that the moment he kills you, I'm going to kill him.''

Phat smiled. "You don't understand,'' he said. "I don't care about my life.''

Hunter smiled back. "No, asshole, *you* don't

understand. I don't care about the lieutenant's life.'' Hunter raised his M-16.

Cox's eyes grew wide with terror. He started to shout an order, but the words died in his mouth as he heard the explosion of Phat's pistol. He never felt the bullet crash into his head, nor did he live long enough to see Sergeant Hunter Two Bears fire a burst of ten rounds into Phat's chest.

Hunter turned and walked back through his squad. They were all standing now and they looked at him and at the lieutenant as if they couldn't believe what they had just seen. Finally Pepper shrugged.

''Fuck it,'' he said philosophically.

''Really,'' someone anwered.

''Let's get breakfast,'' another put in.

# Epilogue

*Pine Ridge Indian Reservation, 1986*

After several miles of rolling hills, they came into a little town. On the surface of it, the little town wasn't that different from any other town in this part of the country. It was one long main street, with stores and houses on both sides of the street. There were two service stations, a police-fire station, a little park, and a school. The truck stopped in front of the school and the policeman walked back to the van.

"You'll find him here someplace," the policeman said. "He's a janitor for the school."

"A janitor? But, doesn't he get a retirement?"

The policeman shook his head no. "He didn't get his twenty. He left at eighteen years."

"What? Why?"

"Nobody knows. He doesn't talk about it."

The policeman's radio came alive and the policeman held up his hand. "I gotta go," he said. "You'll find Hunter around here somewhere."

"Thanks," Ernie said. He watched the policeman drive off. Then he walked up the walk toward the school building. He pushed the doors open and stepped inside. Although it was summertime, there were two young people just inside, a boy and a girl.

"Excuse me," Ernie said. "Could you tell me where I might find Hunter Two Bears?"

"Out back, shootin' V.C.," the boy said derisively.

"Danny!" the girl protested. "Don't talk about him like that. He's an old man."

*He's old? What does that make me?* Ernie wondered.

"He's strange," the boy said. "They got his Distinguished Service Cross in a glass case down at the police station, but there's no way you're going to make me believe that old man won that."

"Believe it," Ernie said.

"Yeah? All I've ever seen him do is push a broom around and drink."

"Be glad that's all you ever saw him do," Ernie said. He walked through the entry hall, then across the basketball court, then through a door at the back of the building. He saw someone near the back of the lot, working on the fence.

It was an old man, with stooped shoulders, and a weathered face. He was wearing jeans and a red T-shirt. Ernie was going to ask him if he knew where to find Hunter Two Bears. . . . Then he saw that it *was* Hunter Two Bears. He walked toward him.

Hunter heard him coming and he looked up. Ernie saw the recognition in his eyes, though Hunter's face made no change.

"Saw where you retired," Hunter said by way of greeting. "Wondered if you'd ever get out this way."

"I told you I would."

Hunter tacked a wire into place with a staple gun. Then he put the tool down and wiped his hands.

"Lot of guys said they would," Hunter said. "You the only one ever did. Let's go somewhere and sit down."

"How about my van?" Ernie offered.

"Okay."

"Why didn't you go until you retired?" Ernie asked, as they walked back through the gym, then back down the walk to Ernie's van.

"I don't know. After Vietnam it wasn't my army anymore," Hunter said. "I didn't know those guys. I didn't belong."

"But you only had two years," Ernie protested. "Two years is so short a time."

"You ever held your hand over a lighted candle?" Hunter asked.

"No."

"Two seconds is a long time."

"Here it is," Ernie said.

"Nice. I see you got a bed fixed up in it and everything."

"Yeah. I've been doing a lot of traveling lately. The van is the best way to do it if you aren't in any particular hurry."

"You're not in any hurry?"

"I figure I have the rest of my life," Ernie answered.

"Have you seen the monument? The one they built in Washington?"

"Yes."

"I'd like to see it. Don't know if I'll ever get the money to make the trip, but I'd like to see it. I'd like to see Bill's name there. Did you see Bill's name?"

"Yes," Ernie said.

"I'd like to sort of reach out and touch his name," he said. "If I could do that, maybe I could close a few old wounds. Maybe I wouldn't . . ." — he took a deep breath — ". . . maybe I wouldn't see Lieutenant Cox's eyes anymore."

"I have something for you," Ernie said. He opened a drawer in a little chest in his van and pulled out a brown leather briefcase. He unsnapped it, then removed a piece of paper.

"What's that?"

"It's a rubbing of Bill's name," Ernie said. "I made it off the monument."

"I'll be a son of a bitch." Hunter reached out and touched the paper. "How about that?"

"Do you want it?" Ernie asked.

"What? No . . . I mean, it's yours. I couldn't take it."

"I did it for you," Ernie said.

Hunter picked it up and held it, almost reverently. "You did?"

"Yeah, I did. Go on, take it."

They were silent for a long moment. A wisp of smoke passed through the van and Ernie caught the unmistakable aroma of barbecued steaks.

"Who's cooking steaks?" Ernie asked.

"The B.I.A.," Hunter said. "They're having a big feed this afternoon for the reservation officers."

"Sounds nice."

"Yeah, if you're an officer."

Ernie smiled. "I seem to recall that not being an officer didn't keep us from eating their steaks the last time the three of us were together." He nodded toward the paper rubbing of Bill Hanlon's name.

Hunter laughed. "No, and, by God, it won't this time," he said. "Let me just make a little recon here. I'll be back in a few minutes."

"I'll furnish the beer," Ernie offered.

**JOHN BALL**
AUTHOR OF **IN THE HEAT OF THE NIGHT** INTRODUCING, **POLICE CHIEF JACK TALLON** IN THESE EXCITING, FAST-PACED MYSTERIES.

## WESTERNS

____ **BUNCH GRASS** — Chuck Harrigan wanted
peace — but he'd have to start a war to get it!
**7701-0515-7/$2.95**

____ **GUNPLAY VALLEY** — A wealthy cattleman turns
a peaceful land into a flaming valley of death.
**7701-0551-3/$2.95**

____ **THE LONG WIND** — Dawson rides off the wind-
swept prairie into a fiery war!

**7701-0449-5/$2.95**

____ **RETURN OF THE KID** — A small town becomes
the battleground for a very deadly family
feud. **7701-0623-4/$2.95**

Available at your local bookstore or return this coupon to:

# FREE!!
# BOOKS BY MAIL
# CATALOGUE

BOOKS BY MAIL will share with you our current bestselling books as well as hard to find specialty titles in areas that will match your interests. You will be updated on what's new in books at no cost to you. Just fill in the coupon below and discover the convenience of having books delivered to your home.

*PLEASE ADD $1.00 TO COVER THE COST OF POSTAGE & HANDLING.*

- - - - - - - - - - - - - - - - - - - - - - - - - - -

**BOOKS BY MAIL**
320 Steelcase Road E.,
Markham, Ontario L3R 2M1

IN THE U.S. -
210 5th Ave., 7th Floor
New York, N.Y., 10010

Please send Books By Mail catalogue to:

Name _____
(please print)

Address _____

City _____

Prov./State _____ P.C./Zip _____
(BBM1)